SAM CRESCENT

EVERNIGHT PUBLISHING ®

www.evernightpublishing.com

SAM CRESCENT

DEDICATION

Writing is such a pleasure for me and I love bringing characters together. Without Evernight Publishing, Devil's Charm wouldn't have a home and as always I'm thankful to them for taking my biker books.

Also, my readers, you all make writing such a joy. I hope you all love Devil like I do.

SAM CRESCENT

DEVIL'S CHARM

Chaos Bleeds, 1

Sam Crescent

Copyright © 2014

Prologue

"What the hell are you doing, Kayla? You can't leave him here," Lexie Howard said, glancing down at the baby who couldn't have been more than a few weeks old.

"You're my sister, and we both know you'll handle this a hell of a lot better than I would." Kayla handed over a bag filled with all kinds of crap a newborn needed. "I've got everything here. His food, clothes, diapers. Oh, and here is some money to tide you over."

Taking the envelope from her older sister Lexie looked inside to see well over ten thousand dollars.

"Fuck, Kayla. What the hell have you been doing?" Lexie stared at the baby then at her sister. Kayla was a beautiful woman, slender with long, silky blonde hair. She'd admired her older sister for as long as she could remember. They were half-sisters as they didn't share the same dad.

"Nothing. It's what I'm due."

Lexie watched as her sister started to head out of the door.

"Wait, you can't just leave me like this with a baby and no fucking clue when you're going to get back."

"His name is Simon. You'll be better for him. I can't look after a baby." Kayla raised her arm showing the track marks of her addiction.

"You said you were getting clean. You can't do this to me. I'm only just surviving myself. There's no work for me to take care of a baby."

"I've given you all of his paperwork. I'm really sorry, but I can't be around. If someone comes calling for me and asking questions promise me you won't say anything. It's better for you and Simon not to say anything."

Following Kayla out of the apartment Lexie felt her whole world crashing around her. At twenty-one years old she couldn't believe she had a little baby in her life.

"This is wrong. I shouldn't take him at all."

"Then I'll be back for him soon. You've just got to keep him by your side and love him. I know you can do that. We're different like that," Kayla said, tears glinting in her eyes. "I can't love him, Lex. You're the only one I've got who'll give him a good home."

Before she could say anything more, Kayla climbed into a beat up car with a guy who looked way too pale to be driving. *Shit.* Lexie charged toward the car only to meet dust. Staring up and down the beat up street, Lexie realized she was alone. She was all alone with a baby who should be with his mother.

"What are you staring at?" she asked the old lady who hadn't moved on from their scene.

She lived in a rundown neighborhood that had long since been forgotten by any government funding. Heading upstairs, she heard Simon screaming. Lexie ran to her apartment, slammed the door closed, and went to the little carrier where her new charge lay. His face was screwed up, and the cries were deafening.

Her next door neighbor slammed their fist against the wall demanding they shut the fuck up. How had her life changed so fucking quickly? One moment she'd been getting ready for work; in the next, she had a baby to look after.

Lifting Simon out of the carrier she held him close and was shocked when he grew silent staring up at her. His eyes were a beautiful blue color, shocking in their appearance and so startling they made her melt instantly.

"Hello, little guy. I'm your Auntie Lexie." Stroking a finger down his cheek, she fell instantly in love. She'd always loved children and babies, recalling all the times she'd babysat for the kids in the surrounding area when she'd been younger. "It looks like I'm going to be taking care of you. I promise to be nice at all times."

Fuck, she didn't know the first thing about looking after a baby. Blowing hair out of her eyes, she carried him over to the kitchen where her second-hand fridge stood. Opening it up she saw the few items of cheap food she owned. Going back to his bags, she started going through everything with one hand.

The moment she tried to put Simon down he screamed. For the next couple of days she'd grow accustomed to what to do. There was nothing else she could do.

Lexie put his things away making a note of the formula he used along with the diapers and creams. When she was finished, she carried him to the nearest store to have a look at what everything was going to cost.

By the time she left the store the tears were threatening to fill her eyes. There was no way she could afford to have a baby. The other problem she faced was in the last few hours she had come to love Simon. It was the strangest feeling in the world. She didn't know this child in any way, yet all of her mothering instincts were coming through begging for her to take care of him. Pushing hair out of her eyes, she stared down into his sleeping face.

"There has got to be something I can do."

The following day she headed out to work, but arriving at the diner with a baby in tow got her fired. Lexie would never forget the look on the woman's face when she walked in with Simon on her hip. She was fired on the spot.

Great, one day with a kid and she'd been fired.

After applying for three jobs with Simon close to her, Lexie knew there was no hope of her getting work.

Going to the end of the street she was caught by the sign for "help wanted" as she passed. The sun was still up, and she wasn't looking at where she was going. Opening the door, she went in and was overcome by a cloud of smoke. Covering Simon's eyes, she gasped as a woman danced naked on the stage semi-naked.

"Can I help you?"

She turned to see a large man with his hair pulled back in a ponytail staring down at her.

"No, I, erm, no, I'm in the wrong place." She made to leave, but he gripped her arm.

"Are you looking for a job?"

Simon was in her arms, and she noticed the man didn't pull too hard on her arm.

"Yes, I was hoping for some waitressing work."

"Anyone look after the kid?" he asked.

She shook her head. "There's only me. I'm all he has."

"Follow me."

With no other choice she followed the large man

to the back where his office was. Lexie couldn't believe she'd walked into a strip club. She hadn't been looking, and desperation was clawing at her for something good to happen.

"I'm Vincent. I own this club."

"I was looking to waitress or bartend or something," she said, holding onto Simon tightly.

Kayla, when we see each other I'm going to fucking kill you.

His gaze wandered down her body. She knew there wasn't much to look at. Lexie wasn't a beautiful woman. Her tits were too large with too wide hips. Her mother loved to tell Lexie how inadequate she was at being a woman. No man wanted a fuller woman in their bed. She didn't possess striking blonde hair but a dull brown that failed to stand out.

"I've lost one of my girls. She was stupid and got herself knocked up. None of my customers want a pregnant woman dancing. Otherwise they'd stay home and look at their wives." Biting her lip, Lexie tried not to take offence. "You're looking good for just giving birth."

"He's not mine. My sister has left him with me while she sorts out her problems." Lexie thought of the thousands of dollars her sister had left her. She knew that money wasn't Kayla's. The last thing she wanted to do was use money she didn't trust.

"That explains it. Do you dance well?"

"I can't be a stripper," she said.

He glared. "Why not? You too good or something?"

"No, look at me. I can't get my clothes off. I'm not exactly stripper material." She poked at her rounded stomach.

"Give me the boy."

"What?" she asked, tightening her arms once

again.

"I'm willing to hire you. Pass me the boy. I won't hurt him. I own a strip club. I ain't no child killer."

Licking her lips, heart pounding, she passed Simon into the man's arms. She was surprised when he settled.

"I've got kids of my own, honey. I know how to hold a kid." Vincent made sure Simon was settled before turning his attention back to her. "Take your shirt off."

She hesitated, staring at him.

"I'm not going to hurt you, but I need to make sure I'm right."

Need the money. You're doing this for Simon.

Lifting up her shirt, she closed her eyes waiting for him to say something.

"Take your jeans off. I need to see what I'm working with."

With her eyes still closed she removed her jeans standing before him in only her bra and panties.

"Turn around."

Lexie turned around knowing his gaze was sliding up and down her body assessing her for work.

"Good, I've got some nice girls who'll be happy to show you how to work the pole. They're not feeding an addiction either."

She stared down at Vincent, who was cooing at Simon.

"What?" she asked. "I would be bad for business."

"You're not a skinny bitch with your ribs showing, but you're what I'm looking for. Men love to see a variety of women, and with those tits and ass you'd earn some decent tips from the men. Get the right song and you'll be one great dancer."

"I'm fat."

Vincent laughed. "You women today. I don't know who declares someone fat or not, but for me, you're just right. Get dressed, and you can start on Friday. Until then you can come by and train."

Like that, Lexie got dressed and was hired as a dancer. She'd never been so shocked in all of her life.

Chapter One

Six months later

Lexie stared at her reflection in the mirror hating every part of herself as she couldn't find a single reason to walk out of the door. For six months she'd been dancing at Naked Fantasies. Vincent, her boss, wasn't a bad man, but he expected the best of his girls. When she hadn't been able to eat for several weeks he'd not liked it and ordered her to eat. He must be the only man in living history who forced one of his strippers to eat food to remain the same shape.

"What are you moping about?" Jenny asked, taking a seat beside her. Jenny was one of the few women Lexie had grown close to. She was a sweet girl with a child of her own. Her husband loved the fact he'd married a stripper and was one of their regular customers.

"Nothing, just thinking about going out there."

Jenny had taught her how to use the pole without killing herself.

"The men love you, honey. Vincent is worried about you. He's not like a lot of strip club owners. I know, it's where I started out," Jenny said, reaching out to touch her arm.

"What do you mean?" Lexi asked, pushing her hair out of the way. She wore a blonde wig, which irritated her.

"Some owners make us give extra. They have VIP rooms where a lot of shit goes on. Vincent is above board. Anything extra is between the girls and the clients. If a guy wants a blow job, then the girl can give it on her own, but she doesn't have to."

On the way out of the club Lexie had seen her fair

share of men getting their dicks swallowed by some of the dancers. In the last six months she'd stumbled on more sex acts than she had in her twenty-one years. She wasn't a virgin. Her lame ass boyfriend at the tender age of sixteen had taken care of that. Lexie was just thankful he'd not given her anything bad or put a baby inside her. Growing up trying to fend for herself there was no room for a child.

"I know I've got a good thing going. I just hate it at times. Sorry, Simon kept me up all night. He slept all day, and it was hard to settle him."

"When is your sister coming back for him?"

"I don't know. I've not heard from her since she dropped him off. I've not got a clue what to do."

Jenny smiled. "Keep doing what you're doing."

"Hey, fatty, you're up next." Tiffany, one of the tiniest girls she'd ever seen, stumbled into the room. The girl was a known user, and Lexie had stumbled onto the girl shooting up between slots. Vincent went crazy when he found her. He didn't like drugs on his property.

"Fuck off, slut," Jenny said. "Go and find your crack dealer to suck off."

"Fuck you, bitch."

Tiffany stumbled away.

"Thank you." Lexie smiled even as the woman's insults hit too close to home for her.

"Anytime, baby. I can't stand that slut. She's a fucking menace and will end up dead od'ing or something. Go on, get out there and kill it."

Rising out of the chair, Lexie squealed as Jenny slapped her ass.

For the next ten minutes she blocked out the crowd as she wrapped her body around the pole. She'd not become strong enough to ride up and down the pole, but she worked her body to the music.

Over the months Lexie preferred to think of herself as having one man to dance to. In her mind she imagined someone in a suit who was in control of everything. He'd stare at her without losing his cool but knowing he was loving every second of her dance. Her imaginary man helped her through.

When it was over she walked down the steps leaving the men and the stage behind. Vincent was waiting for her.

"What is going on with you?" he asked, escorting her toward his office.

She quickly put her shirt on hoping her body was covered away from prying eyes.

"I'm working."

He slammed the door closed, glaring at her. "Are you using?" Vincent lifted her arms checking to see if there was needle marks in her flesh.

"What? Hell, no. I'm not using anything." He gripped her face, lifting her head up to look up her nose. "Stop it. I'm not using anything, okay. I'm just fucking tired."

"Kid keeping you up?" he asked.

"Yes, he's keeping me up. I'm doing the best I can."

"The men love you. You're a great dancer, Lexie. I need you to keep your shit about you."

She shook her head. "Are you a saint or something?"

"I'm a father. I need to make sure that boy is taken care of."

He couldn't have shocked her more. "I wouldn't do anything to hurt Simon. Why couldn't you be less of a pain in the ass?" she asked.

"Easy, I'm not your standard fucking club owner. I work this club for a friend."

"Okay. I'm sorry for worrying you."

After a few seconds he let her go. Heading back around to the changing rooms she sat in the toilet, heaving up the food she'd eaten. Fuck, she couldn't handle this lifestyle.

"I can't believe they're here. I've been waiting for them to get back into town. It has been over two years, and wow, Devil is still as hot as I remembered," Tiffany said, no longer sounding high.

Lifting her legs off the floor, Lexie tried to ignore them. She didn't want anyone to know she was in the toilet.

Diana was with her, giggling. "I love Death. His name is scary, but he fucks better than Pussy."

Covering her ears, Lexie didn't want to hear anything. There was no mistaking what they were doing when she heard them inhale deeply. Glancing through the small slit in the door, in the mirror she saw both girls snorting coke. If Vincent was to find them, he'd hurt them real bad. He didn't like drugs in his strip club.

"God, I can't wait to suck cock. I tell you, I hate those fuckers drooling over me for a couple of bucks, but Devil, he knows how to treat me," Tiffany said, rubbing her nose. "That's good. It'll keep me going for a while."

"Come on, let's get out there."

Within minutes they were gone taking their giggling with them.

Lexie stayed in the toilet, wiping away her tears.
I'm doing this for Simon. I'm doing this for Simon.

In that moment, Lexie really hated her sister and her entire upbringing. Their mother had been more interested in the bottle and men than in her daughters. Lexie had gotten through school with good grades but not enough to win any kind of scholarship. Kayla dropped out of school, and by the time Lexie left at eighteen she was already working every hour she could.

"Lex, honey, you in here?" Jenny asked.

Opening the stall she stared at her friend who carried the cheap makeup bag.

"You're on in twenty. We need to fix you up."

Standing still she let Jenny do her makeup restoring back her night face for the men.

"I heard Tiffany and Diane talking about some group that entered."

Jenny tensed. "They've taken over the whole club, kicking everyone out. When Chaos Bleeds come in, then no one else is allowed around."

"Chaos Bleeds? Is it some kind of rock group?"

"No, I wish. They're a motorcycle club. Tough men with no rules, and every now and then they come to town. Devil is the leader," Jenny said.

"I don't like the sound of this group."

"Take my advice, do your set, get your money and fucking leave. You do not want to get embroiled with these men. They're dangerous, and they carry."

Lexie nodded. "I'm not interested in getting anything."

Vincent appeared in the doorway. "Come on. Get your ass up on the stage."

"I'm going." She looked at Jenny, who looked at her.

"You're good. Go and kick ass. I wish I had your tits. So fucking big." Jenny grabbed her own making Lexie laugh.

She knew Jenny was just putting her at ease. "I'll see you after, right?"

"Yes, hubby is coming to get me in an hour, and then I'm off."

"This is your last set for tonight, Lex. You can

leave when you're done," Vincent said, leaving the bathroom.

"I'll wait for you before I leave."

"Appreciate it. Go on, knock them dead."

Heading out of the toilet she walked down to the back of the stage as the lights were turned off over the seating area. The only light would be on her.

In the mirror she checked her blonde wig making sure not a strand of her brown hair showed.

You can do this. Simply dance, imagine your suit man.

The music started, and it was one of her favorites. Wrapping her arms around the pole she waited for the light to appear on her, and then she started to work the pole how Jenny had shown her.

****

Devil, leader of the Chaos Bleeds MC and an irritated man, swallowed back a shot of the whiskey. Business had been booming at Naked Fantasies since he'd last come to town. Wiping a hand down his face, he felt fucking tired. He was getting too old to be chasing shit around town. At forty-five years old he knew it was time for him to settle down rather than have to deal with riding from place to place. His men were getting tired of the same old shit, and he was starting to want a nice warm bed to sleep in at night. He refused to believe it was down to his aging years.

For the last twenty years he'd done nothing but ride. His group had the same need in their blood to be free and not controlled by the social convention. If he wanted to fuck three women, one after the other, then he fucking did it. He transported drugs and drank until he vomited. There was no such thing as a happy hour to him. Every hour was fucking happy hour. If he wanted a drink at ten in the morning, he'd have a drink.

"Hey, baby, I missed you."

Tiffany, one of the dancers and a huge slut, walked toward him. There was white powder around her nose showcasing her expensive habit. Whenever he came around he always lost himself in her body. She was so fucking skinny, and since the last time he'd been back she looked thinner. Any arousal vanished as he caught sight of her ribcage. Why did women think it was fucking sexy to see every fucking bone in their body?

"Fuck off," he said, not wanting any company. He needed to think. Kayla had been a fucking mistake. The condom he'd used had broken, and afterward he'd gotten himself tested. He liked being free, but he didn't want to die from some fucking disease. Getting a clean bill of health he later found out the slut was pregnant with his child and then after that she'd given birth. The bitch had also stolen over ten thousand dollars from him. Once he got his kid away from her then she was going to find herself a nice comfortable bed to die in. No one took the piss out of him and got away from it.

"Devil, I'll do anything," Tiffany said. "Please, I've missed you."

She started to rub at his lap, and his cock stiffened. He'd not had a good fuck in a long time. Tiny and The Skulls had been accommodating, but he'd wanted to taste that sweet Angel, Lash's woman. Lash didn't believe in sharing, not that Devil took offence. If he had a woman like Angel, he wouldn't want to share her either.

"Take my dick out and suck it," he said. If she was going to start working his cock the least she could do was suck it.

Down Tiffany went under the table pulling out his length.

"Hey, mate," Vincent said, approaching the table.

Shaking hands with the man he'd left to run the strip club, Devil found Tiffany's mouth less than appealing. Still, it was better than looking at the bitch. "What brings you back here?"

"I'm looking for someone. I'll tell you about it in the morning. For now, I just want to enjoy a few minutes relaxing. Who's next?" he asked, nodding toward the stage.

"A new dancer, Lexie. You'll like her."

He was looking for a woman named Lexie. Devil tensed, wondering if by sheer luck the woman he was looking for was the same woman on the stage. It couldn't be. His life wasn't about sheer luck. There was no way the woman he was hunting for would be the same woman.

Sinking his fingers into Tiffany's hair, he forced her to take all of his length, to swallow around the tip of his cock. Tiffany took him without question, sucking on his length.

"Here she is now."

The stage lit up, and Devil's interest was piqued. The woman on the stage was not like any of the other girls they employed. For one, she was much fuller than the woman between his legs. Her shape was clearly outlined in the corset she wore. Her hips flared out, and the stocking and suspenders went right to his dick. The black and pink set made her look sensual and innocent at the same time.

His cock thickened more at the sight of the woman on the dance floor. The blonde hair reminded him a little of Angel. When he'd seen that sweet beauty he had wanted to start a war with The Skulls, but he'd seen the love she had for Lash and decided against it. The woman on stage turned around, and he saw her face was as beautiful as the rest of her. Forgetting her face, he glanced down her body to see the size of her tits. Fuck, he wanted to bury his head in that rack and see her bouncing above his cock.

Speeding up Tiffany's movements, he watched the woman before him tease all of the men. Her gaze stared blindly out into the audience. She looked far away. Her body swayed to the music, and he knew she didn't give a fuck about the men out of her own little world.

Slowly, she started to work off her kit. Her full, curvy body worked the room. He knew every single man was horny and wanted to see her tits naked. Devil was getting fucking horny just to have a look at her.

When the corset finally came off, Devil erupted filling Tiffany's mouth with his cum as he got off on the woman on stage. Her tits were fucking beautiful. They were ripe, with large red tipped nipples. She worked down the pole, spreading her legs and showing the men her covered pussy.

All too soon the song ended, the stage went blank, and the entire crowd was in uproar. They wanted to see all of the goods. Tiffany climbed out from under the table, wiping his cum away from her mouth.

"She always leaves men wanting more. It's why she gets regular customers hoping for a glimpse at her," Vincent said.

"I want to meet her," Devil said, standing up and adjusting his cock.

"What? I just sucked your dick. You can't do that." Tiffany had her hands on hips as she glared at him.

Grabbing her arm, he hauled her up close. "Don't think for a second you have any fucking claim over me. You're good for one thing and one thing only, to be available for me to fuck. Get out of here, fucking crack-whore."

He threw her off him, looking at Vincent. Tiffany

crashed to the ground, and no one helped her up. She was a whore and was only looking for a man to keep her in coke. He didn't mind being around drugs, but he didn't take the shit himself. Some of his men had lost their lives taking shit, and he asked them to keep their habit in fucking check.

Being on the open road with no rules meant he couldn't screw up other peoples wants either. Drug taking was not on his list, but he asked his men to keep it together.

"Follow me. She'll be leaving soon."

Vincent took him around to the dressing rooms as another woman came on stage. His men were surrounded by women. Devil knew when they came to town, women flocked to them.

"Lex, we're coming in. A friend wants to meet you." Vincent opened the door, and they found her putting on some jeans. The sexy corset had been replaced by a simple cotton bra. Devil wanted to cry at the sin of putting those babies away.

"What can I do for you, Vincent? You said I only had to dance."

Her voice was so fucking sweet. He'd been on the road too long listening to women with attitudes who were a bit long in the tooth and too long into the lifestyle. This woman was fresh faced and … young. He'd not expected her to be so young. She couldn't be older than twenty if that.

"Devil wanted to meet you."

Walking into the room he realized how small she actually was. Her head only came to his chest.

"I don't do any extras."

"I'm not after extras. You can go, Vincent." He didn't wait for the man to say anything. Vincent left leaving him alone with the stunning woman with big tits.

He reached out surprised when she flinched away from him. "I'm not going to hurt you."

"Okay." She looked doubtful even though she didn't pull away.

Did she have a man who beat her?

"Is there someone waiting for you? A husband, boyfriend?"

"No, no one." She started to bite her lip, stuttering.

"I'm not going to hurt you at all." He pushed some hair off her shoulder, caressing her cheek. She was heavily made up with makeup. Devil didn't like it. He wanted to know what she looked like without all the artifice.

Bending down, he brushed her lips with his as he gripped her ass, drawing her closer. She was tense against him. His cock hardened, wanting inside her tight, hot body.

"What will it take to make you mine for the night?" he asked. All of his men would be envious of him for getting this hot little piece for the night.

Her body grew tenser if that was even possible. "I'm not a whore. I'm not for sale."

She struggled in his arms. He lifted her up with ease, putting her on top of the vanity unit Vincent supplied for the girls to get dressed. She gasped, and he tilted her head back to look at him. "Everyone has a price. What's yours?" He claimed her lips, sliding his tongue into her mouth.

Within minutes she melted against him. The hands that had been pushing him away, gripped him tightly, wanting him. His dick wanted inside her so fucking bad.

Pressing against her hard, Devil wanted all of her clothes off and to sink into her sweetness. Cupping one of her tits he teased the nipple loving the feel of it budded against his palm. She was going to be so fucking hot to claim. He wanted his dick inside her, and he'd even forgo the condom to feel her naked cunt.

"Boss, we need you out here. Ripper is causing some fucking problems," Curse said, grabbing his attention.

Devil pulled away from her, staring into her eyes. "Don't go anywhere. I'll be right back."

Leaving Lexie behind Devil went to deal with one of his men. His thoughts were not on the job at hand only the woman he wanted to fuck.

Chapter Two

What the hell was that all about? Lexie quickly removed her wig, grabbed her bag, and headed outside. Jenny was stood with her husband, giggling as she exited the back of the club.

"I was wondering where you got to. I'll see you in a few days, okay?" Jenny asked.

Nodding, she said goodbye to her friends and headed out into the night. It was late, and she needed to get home to collect her son—Simon. She found herself more and more forgetting that Simon wasn't hers. They'd been together six months so far, but it had started to feel like a lifetime. Every dance and performance she did was one step closer to making a better life for them. She paid the rent and got enough food to feed them both. After buying the necessities for him she tried to earn enough to give him toys and clothes. She even wanted to move out of the crummy apartment to somewhere nice. Listening to couples fuck and fight was not the kind of life she wanted Simon to grow up in.

There was so much she wanted to give him, and yet she struggled day after day to provide for him. Pulling the band out of her hair, she let her hair fall free. After wearing a wig she loved to feel the fresh air. Grabbing the pepper spray out of her bag, she kept on walking feeling a little protected even though it was stupid. Any man could easily overpower her if he chose.

Keeping her head bowed she got to her apartment building with ease. Several women, whores, were working on the streets waiting for a paying customer. She hated this lifestyle. Some of them gave her a nod as she passed. Lexie never judged them for earning money, and several liked her as she took care of their kids when they really needed it.

"Rough night, Lex?" Carol asked. She'd been a whore all of her life, and at thirty something she'd seen it all. Lexie took care of her kids during the night sometimes when money was tight for her.

"Yeah, you could say that. You?"

"Slow. Not many men looking for love tonight."

Smiling, Lexie nodded. "Take care."

"You're way too fucking sweet to be around here." Carol shook her head looking sad.

Lexie got that a lot, but none of these women knew how she'd grown up. This kind of stuff was what she was used to. It made her laugh sometimes that she was more used to people selling their bodies than helping her out at the grocery store.

"See you tomorrow," Lexie said, heading up.

Simon was with Jessica on the floor above her. When Lexie knocked on the door, Jessica answered at the third knock. "Hey, I was wondering if you were coming back."

"Sorry. Is he okay?" Lexie entered the apartment to see Simon asleep on the sofa.

"Yeah, he's been perfect. A good little boy you got there."

"Thank you." Grabbing some notes from her pocket she handed them over. "I really appreciate you looking after him."

"No problem. Same again next week?"

"Yeah." Picking Simon up, she walked down to her own apartment unlocking the door and entering. He didn't wake up, which she was pleased about. After the last couple of days she really needed her beauty sleep. She was dead on her feet, and she knew Vincent would fire her ass if she looked less than appealing tomorrow night. Locking the door, she dropped her bag by the wall and walked into her bedroom.

She'd bought a second hand cot and scrubbed it raw before she put him into it. The mattress was new. Laying him down, she watched him sleep for several seconds before heading for the shower.

Within twenty minutes she was tucked up in bed listening to the noises all around her. The couple on her right was screwing again. She listened to the bed hitting the wall, their groans combining together as they neared release.

They quieted down, and she wondered if that would be all for the night. Some of the men seemed to catch their breaths and be back humping away within minutes. She listened to the noise outside as cars pulled up and drove away. Lexie hoped Carol was okay. Out of all the women Carol was one of the nicest.

In a matter of minutes she heard the couple on the right at it again. She wanted to scream at them that quality was better than quantity.

Listening to them going at it reminded Lexie of her own lost virginity. In fact all the times she slept with her boyfriend she couldn't recall any kind of pleasure at all. He'd climb on, thrust a few times, and his face would go weird before it was all over. Not once had she felt any kind of desire or need. *Tonight I did.*

Rolling over, she closed her eyes hoping for sleep to claim her. Instead she saw a man with graying hair at the temples with really intense dark brown eyes. Devil, what kind of name was that? It had to be a road name or something made up. No one named their kid Devil.

His hands had felt so good on her body. The way he picked her up and placed her on the vanity table would stay with her forever. She had felt a pull deep inside at his possessiveness. Was it possessive?

Would she have fucked him? If they'd not been interrupted Lexie knew she wouldn't have been able to fight him at all. There was something magnetic about him. His gaze saw far more than he let on.

Get over yourself. No man sees anything but his dick.

She turned over to look at Simon. He was the only thing she needed to be thinking about. Other men could go and fuck themselves. She didn't need anyone or anything. Climbing out of the bed she walked over to the window to look out at the night sky. It was dark and all the stars were shining brightly. At that moment she really hoped wishes could be true. She'd wish for a much better life for Simon.

Closing her eyes, she headed back to bed, resting her head on the pillow. Within minutes sleep finally claimed her.

****

The club had turned into a fucking orgy. Devil watched the room seeing all of his men in different states of undress as women attended to their every need. Vincent sat at the bar with him nursing a beer.

"Missed you on the road," Devil said. Vincent had been one of their crew for a long time. When he'd fallen for a little redhead with lips that looked like they could pleasure a man, Vincent had bowed out of the road. He was still a member of the Chaos Bleeds, but he looked after the strip club rather than ride. It worked out well, as Devil hated to bring outsiders into club life.

"I missed the road, but I know I'd miss Phoebe more. She's my world, man."

"You sound like a whipped pussy." Sipping at his beer, Devil glanced toward the girls' changing rooms. The bitch he'd wanted for the night was long gone. She'd taken off while he dealt with Ripper and Spider's problem. His two boys had been fighting over a woman. Looking toward them Devil got angry. Why fight over a woman and then fucking share her anyway? It made no sense to him.

"I am. No one compares to her at all."

"How does she find you running a strip club? Does she check your dick out for lipstick marks?"

"She knows I wouldn't screw anything here. They're here to earn money, and half of them are probably STD riddled." Vincent shook his head. "I don't know how it happened, but I'm a one woman man now. I know, pussy, right?"

"Nah, I saw some of The Skulls. They're the same. Looked happy and I'm happy for you." Devil slapped his friend on the back.

"How long you sticking around for this time?" Vincent asked.

"Worried we'll upset your woman?"

"Nah, Phoebe doesn't have a problem with you guys. You're family, and she's big on family."

"The boys are looking to settle down. We can do our runs and shit, but crashing in dives has lost its appeal." Devil took another sip of his beer. "We're looking to have a little thing going like Tiny. He's got a fucking dream up and running. No one gives him shit, beside the obvious problems of the club. I was thinking we could do something here. Build a club and earn money."

"You'd have to get rid of the pimps or strike up a deal. Some of the men love their women earning money," Vincent said.

"Any trouble here?"

"Only when one of them tried to take my girls. I don't like unwilling, and believe me when I say I've got a couple of girls unwilling to trade stripping for whoring." Vincent threw the empty bottle into the trash can.

"Like who?" Devil asked.

"Jenny, she's the short one. Sweet, husband comes in every night to see her shows. They've got a thing going, and I think they're only here to spice up their love life." Vincent chuckled. "He's the one who stayed 'round the back. Always taking care of his woman."

"Sounds like a club man."

"Probably. He only wants Jenny though."

"The other?" Devil asked, hoping Lexie's name came up. Shit, he really needed to look for Kayla's sister. She could be his only hope of finding his son.

"Lexie is the other. She's single from what I know. Came in six months ago needing a job. Insecure though. She only wanted a waitressing job. Thought she was too fat to be a dancer," Vincent said.

"Fucking bitches. I really don't know what goes on in their heads." Devil couldn't be bothered with women talking about dieting and shit. Once they started talking shit, he shoved his dick in their mouth to shut them up.

"Yeah, she's a good earner. The little boy she's looking after is cute, too. She came in with him."

Devil froze. Okay, the name was a fucking coincidence but not that fucking much.

"What the hell you talking about?" Devil asked.

"What's the matter?"

"Start from the beginning. What fucking kid?"

Vincent frowned. "She turned up six months ago carrying a baby. A little boy, newborn. Her sister had showed up and dumped him. Left Lexie to provide for him and that's when she came to me for a job. She sounded pretty desperate."

"You've got to be fucking kidding me." Devil stood up heading toward the office. After his recent phone call with Tiny, he wasn't in the mood to start shit. Hearing about Snitch being back from the fucking dead hadn't put him in a good mood. There was no way he'd been kissing the woman he was looking for. Miracles did not fall into his fucking lap so easily.

"Devil, hold it, what's going on?" Vincent asked.

He opened the filing cabinet where Vincent kept the files of all of their employees. The strip club was aboveboard and fucking legal. No one could slam them with anything. Finding her file, he looked at the man who had her this whole time.

"On the road I knocked up a woman by the name of Kayla Howard. You know her?" Devil asked.

"No, I've never heard of her."

"Her half-sister is known as Lexie Howard. They have different fucking dads but the same mom." He pulled out the information that Tiny had gotten for him off Whizz. The girl in the picture didn't look anything like the woman he had seen tonight.

"Everything matches up. The baby, the time frame, everything," Devil said.

"Are you telling me, Lexie, my stripper, is who you've come looking for?" On the road Devil hadn't phoned with any update or anything for Vincent. He'd simply told the other man he was on his way to see him. "She's a good girl, Devil."

"Her sister is the one I've got a fucking problem with. Where does Lexie live?" he asked, looking through her work.

Vincent took the paperwork from him. "Promise me you're not going to hurt this girl. She's working hard for that boy. He's yours, isn't he?"

"The boy, yeah, he's mine. I'm going to do a fucking paternity test to find out first. Knowing Kayla he could be fathered by anyone."

Devil saw her date of birth put her at twenty-one years old. Kayla was over five years older than she was.

"Tell me I'm not about to put this girl in danger?" Vincent asked.

"I've not got a problem with the girl. She's not a blonde then." He thought about her hair, which reminded him so much of Angel. Part of him was pleased she didn't have blonde hair.

"It's a wig."

Vincent gave him the address. "Do you think you should be going out now?"

"No time like the present. I want to see her now." He headed out of the office. Someone turned the music off as he grabbed his boys' attention. "Anyone who can ride get your asses on your bike. I've got to go and get my kid. Is this place okay for us to crash tonight?" Devil asked. Tomorrow he'd be looking to find a place big enough, like Tiny had. The more he thought about it the more he liked the idea of having all of his men in one place.

"Sure. This is your place, Devil. Deeds are all in your name."

"Good. You can head on home. Send my love to Phoebe."

"Will do. What do you want me to do about the women here?"

"Shit, some of my men can stay while I get this shit sorted out." Devil walked out of the building toward his bike. Straddling his machine, he turned the ignition, loving the feel of the bike coming to life. It was time for him to get to his kid and get him home safe.

Not got a home.

He'd handle all the other finer details later.

The ride didn't take long at all. He was shocked by the activity outside the apartment building. Women stood waiting for some kind of action. In a few hours the sun would be up and the women would disappear. Is this the kind of life Lexie was looking for? He didn't even know the woman, and yet he was pissed at the fact she was living like this.

A pimp was yelling as he thumped one of the girls. Devil hated getting in other people's business, but the girl was already black and blue.

"What are you doing, boss?" Curse asked.

Curse had gotten his name during one of their rides. Whatever could go wrong on the guy's bike had, and they'd nicknamed him Curse. His real name was Bradley James, and he was a damn good man. Devil made sure the men who stuck right by him were not users or abusers. There were some rules he abided by even if he didn't show it to anyone else. He liked the fact The Skulls thought he was ruthless, which he was, but he wasn't into beating up bitches either.

He was all about fair fighting, and a pimp against a scared young girl was not fair. She didn't look all that old either.

"I hate pimps almost as much as I hate liars." Devil clicked his knuckles approaching the man who was kicking the girl on the ground.

"No, please, stop, he didn't pay me. I promise you he didn't pay me." The girl was whimpering, sobbing, and trying to protect herself from the brutish attack.

"You're a fucking slut. Pay me my money." The pimp wouldn't stop.

Clearing his throat, Devil waited for Pimp to stop.

"What the fuck do you want?" Pimp asked.

"What's your name?"

"Rob, what's it the fuck to you?" Rob, the pimp, walked away from the girl to get into Devil's face. "Do you want me to fuck you over, huh?"

Devil's men chuckled.

"You the pimp around here, pretty boy?" Devil asked.

"Yeah, you want to start working on my land you've got to pay a fucking fee. These are my girls, and this is my fucking lan—" Devil slammed his forehead against Rob's. There was only so much shouting he was going to accept. He hated pimps and especially pimps who forced girls into the lifestyle. The girl he'd been beating didn't look older than seventeen. When Rob grabbed his nose, he landed a blow to his face. Rob went down, and he slammed his foot onto the guy's junk for good measure.

Rob screamed like a girl.

He noticed a lot of women were cheering at him for beating on the fucking pimp.

"Now, let's see if I've got this right. I own this place. Name is Devil, and I'm president of Chaos Bleeds."

"Fuck you, prick." Rob made to spit on him.

Pressing Rob's face against the tarmac, Devil waited for him to scream before lifting him up. The girl Rob had been beating on looked, terrified.

"It's time for you to say sorry." Dragging Rob across the ground by his hair toward the girl he saw Curse was talking to her, stopping her from running away. "What's your name, honey?" Devil asked.

"It's Judi."

"How old are you, Judi?"

"I'll be eighteen in three weeks."

"You telling me you're not even eighteen yet?" Devil asked.

"No."

The desire to end Rob was strong, but he needed

him to put the word out about Chaos Bleeds. Once the word was out, Rob was going to be his.

"You will not fucking touch her again. If I see your face around here I will put a bullet through your motherfucking skull. Do you understand me?" Devil asked.

"Yeah, I get it."

"Say sorry," Devil said.

"I'm not saying sorry to that fucking slut."

Rob's hand was flat out on the ground. Lifting his foot, Devil brought it down. He heard the crunch of bone as Rob squealed like a girl.

"I'm sorry. I'm so fucking sorry."

"That wasn't so difficult, was it?" Devil asked. "Get the fuck out of my sight. I see you once more then you're fucking dead."

The pimp scrambled away trying to run so fast.

"Judi, are you okay?" Devil asked, crouching down to look her in the eye.

"Thank you. Thank you so much." She moved to her knees and then wrapped her arms around his neck. The young girl sobbed as her frail body trembled.

"Get her cleaned up. Where's your parents?" Devil asked.

"Gone. They've been gone a long time."

Hating the world, Devil handed her over to Curse, who then handed her to Death. They'd take care of her. Girls her fucking age should be loving life not dealing with shit-heads like Rob. He despised pimps. Women who were not willing shouldn't be forced into any kind of lifestyle.

Shaking his head, Devil headed toward the front of the apartment building.

"Who are you looking for?" a woman in her thirties asked.

"None of your business." He headed into the building and started climbing the floors until he came to the right one.

"Is this girl a whore?" Curse asked.

"No, she's a stripper. Vincent likes her, or at least I think he does."

"He's turned into a pussy with that woman of his."

"I wouldn't tell him that. He'd cut your dick off," Devil said, standing outside the door. He stared at the wooden door knowing it wouldn't stop anyone from getting inside.

"What's the plan?"

"I get in and get my kid."

"So no plan."

Devil shrugged. He'd not thought anything through. Trying the door, he knew it was locked. It was going to need a little more strength behind it.

Chapter Three

After a couple of hours' sleep Lexie was up to attend a screaming Simon. Rubbing the sleep from her eyes, she picked the young boy out of the bed. She changed his diaper and then headed into her small kitchen. The apartment was so small, but it worked for her at the time. It was better than being on the streets.

"I've got you," she said, humming as she warmed him up a new bottle. She was so tired, but he came first.

Walking around the small space she hummed to him as the bottle warmed up. Testing the bottle, she slotted it into his mouth watching him suck on the teat. Suddenly, she tensed as her apartment door was kicked open. The locks were nothing against the brutal force of the two men making their way inside.

She closed her mouth as she saw Devil walk into the room. The other man she recognized from the strip club.

They closed the door, neither speaking as they looked at her. Devil stared at her then at the boy in her arms. She wore a pair of shorts and a vest top. It was a warm night, and wearing anything more would irritate her skin.

"What the hell are you doing?" she asked. Protecting Simon all she could think about. Was this man going to hurt her? Rape her? Kill her? No, no one could hurt her with a baby. Simon couldn't be hurt.

He didn't say a word. The other man leaned against the door smirking at her.

"She's hotter without the blonde wig, Boss. You did fucking good."

"You can't just storm in here. Get the hell out."

Simon fidgeted in her arms. She took several breaths trying to calm her beating heart. There was nothing she could do to defend herself. They had caught her vulnerable. She was always fucking vulnerable, and it was a relief not to have been dragged into anything else before now.

"Kayla Howard, where is she?" Devil asked.

Lexie tensed. "How do you know Kayla?"

He moved to her scabby sofa, sitting down. "Where is she?"

"I don't know. How do you know her?" she asked.

"You're holding my kid."

"What? No, that is not possible." She looked down at Simon and wondered what the hell was going on. Kayla had become mixed up in some serious shit. She didn't want to believe it even as she knew it was the truth.

"Stole money from me as well. I've found one thing that's mine, but she needs to pay for what she's done," Devil said. He stared into her eyes before dropping back down to his boy.

She didn't know what the hell was happening.

"How can you be his father?" she asked.

"Didn't you finish school? I fucked her, condom broke, and he is the consequence." Devil stood, stepping closer to her.

"I know how it happens." Closing her eyes she tried to think around the panic clawing its way inside her. "She never mentioned his father at all."

"Tell me what happened." He stood in front of her with his gaze on Simon.

"She, erm, six months ago she dropped by with him. He was only a couple of weeks old, but she didn't want to take him with her."

"I want to hold him."

Nodding, she passed him over into Devil's arms.

He was so tall and big. Simon curled against him, suckling at his bottle.

"Keep his head supported."

She moved away, rubbing her eyes. Curse was watching her, and she felt the heat of both men's gazes. Hating their attention she turned to the sink washing the few dishes in the sink. Her apartment wasn't much, but she kept it neat and clean.

At the club she was protected from the men by Vincent and his guards, but at her apartment there was nothing to protect her.

Her heart pounded as she turned to look at the large man.

Devil was staring at her.

"You're not a blonde?"

"No, I'm not." She tried to keep her identity a secret so she didn't have any problems away from the strip club. Her makeup was always thick, and her hair was hidden by the blonde wig.

"I need to know where Kayla is," he said.

"Well that makes both of us." Running fingers through her hair she became aware of the fact she wasn't wearing a bra.

"So fucking lucky," Curse said.

"I've not seen her since she handed me Simon." Thinking about the money she went to her fridge and pulled out the envelope she kept inside. "This is what she gave me as well. I don't want any trouble at all. I've not spent a penny."

Devil stared at the envelope then at her.

"I'm not looking for money." He handed Simon back to her. "Finish dealing with him, and then we'll talk."

She wished he would just leave, but then Simon would be gone. Shit, he was going to take Simon away from her.

Finishing his feed and burping him, she put Simon down. He went straight to sleep leaving her alone with two men. Tucking some hair behind her ears she turned to see Devil sitting on the sofa. Curse was by the door, watching her.

"Take a seat." Devil pointed to the seat beside him.

Seeing no other choice, she sat beside him and tucked her legs beneath her. His hand rested on her knee. The touch made her tense at the sensation that crashed over her.

Her pussy felt slick with cream as her clit pulsed. The feeling took her completely by surprise.

Neither of them spoke for a long time.

"Curse, take the boys and go back to the club. I'll be there in the morning."

"Sure thing, Boss. Just to warn you, we're not going to all love sleeping in a strip club for long," Curse said.

"I've already got plans in place. We're not going to be sleeping there all that long."

The door opened and closed. They were now alone with only Simon asleep in his cot.

Devil stared at her without breaking eye contact.

"You left earlier. Did you know who I was?" he asked.

"I had no idea who Kayla was in trouble with. I didn't know who you were, and if I did I would have fucking told you." She was panicking.

"I'm not going to hurt you."

He opened the envelope.

"It's all there."

"You didn't use any of it at all." His hand started to stroke up and then down her thigh.

"I wanted to, but I got a job at Naked Fantasies instead. Kayla has never made the wisest decisions. I didn't want to risk using money that wasn't hers." Running a hand over her face, Lexie really wanted the night to end.

He dropped the envelope beside him on the floor. The air between them changed. It became charged, and she found it hard to breathe as his gaze moved down her body. She felt naked beneath his gaze rather than wearing her night clothes.

"You left before I got a chance to get back." His fingers slid up the inside of her thigh.

"Nothing was going to happen."

Devil reached out, grabbing her around the waist and tugging her onto his lap. "Something was going to happen, baby."

She straddled his waist feeling the hard length of his shaft pressed against her sex.

Staring into Devil's eyes Lexie tried to control the response inside her body. No man should have this kind of hold over her.

"God, your body is to fucking die for." His fingers sank into her hair, drawing her close. She was shocked when he buried his face against her neck inhaling deeply. "Fuck."

Her nipples were so tight they hurt. Thrusting her pelvis on his lap she tried to force her arousal to the back of her mind. The clothing between them felt too rough. His leather jacket covered up his chest.

"Come on, Lex. You know something was going to happen." He gripped her ass holding her steady against his cock. One of his hands moved to cup her pussy. "You're like a bitch in heat."

Lexie didn't say anything. Closing her eyes she let her body dictate to her for once.

You don't know him.

He's dangerous.

There's no way to know what he'll do.

Even with all doubts rushing through her mind the pleasure he was creating with his hands was too much.

"You're fucking hot, baby."

His hand went into her shorts, and Lexie moaned, tensing back up. This was the furthest she'd ever gone with a guy in years. The last guy she'd been with didn't have a clue what he was doing. He certainly never inspired this kind of response from her.

She felt bound up in knots from the pleasure of his touch alone.

Devil separated the lips of her sex sliding down her slit to her entrance. He pushed a finger in deep, and she cried out.

"Fucking tight."

Opening her eyes she lifted up off his lap for him to get deeper.

****

Her cunt was so fucking tight Devil felt like he was in heaven. Pressing a thumb to her clit he watched her face scrunch up as she rode his hand. Her chest was so close to him. He wanted one of her tits. Tugging the vest from her body he admired her rounded breasts. She worked his fingers, and her tits bounced with each thrust.

He couldn't wait to drive his cock deep inside her. She'd drive him over the edge easily.

Lifting her off his lap, he tore off all the clothing stopping him from getting to her body. He loved every curve and wanted to show each part of her attention. Devil tugged her back onto his lap, and she straddled him, opening her pussy against his pants.

Tipping her back to the sofa, he slammed his lips

down on hers claiming the kiss he'd been wanting since he walked through her door. She'd looked so cute with Simon in her arms and her hair tousled. Then he'd grown angry at Kayla passing his kid onto someone else even though he knew Lexie was a better person to look after him. Looking around the small apartment showed she took care.

Life had clearly been hard for her. She'd tensed up expecting the worst from him. He hated the fear in her eyes and would make sure she didn't feel that way with him.

Taking off his jacket, he removed his pants, kicking his boots off in the process. All that remained on was his shirt. He didn't wear underwear. Fisting his length, he was ready to fuck her hard.

He tugged her back onto his lap, getting her to straddle his hips. His naked shaft rested between her slit, bumping her clit. "That's better."

"We can't do this. I don't know you. Shit, what am I doing?"

Devil shut her up by claiming her lips and cupping her ass. She moaned. Her hands cupping his face as she kissed him back. Their tongues danced together, and the fire burned brightly between them. Breaking from her lips he kissed down her neck biting onto her flesh. He wanted to see his mark on her flesh. Down he went until he took one nipple into his mouth. He squeezed her ass, rubbing her pussy up and down the length of his cock. It would be so easy to slide his cock inside her.

Instead he sucked on the hard bud feeling her shake in his hands. Her responses were not controlled. She wasn't used to faking pleasure for men. He knew from her cream leaking over his dick. Lexie loved his touch. Her body awakened more with every second that passed.

Biting down on her nipple to the point of pain he heard her cry out before moving onto the next. He did the same lavishing her breast with attention. They really were magnificent, and he'd always been a tit man.

Her fingers dug into his shoulders. Wrapping his hands around her waist he pressed her back to the sofa, kissing down her body until he lay between her thighs. He never went down on women as he tried to avoid it. The women he'd been with would fuck everything in sight, and the last thing he wanted to do was to be licking out another man's cum.

His boys thought he was crazy to think like that. Devil didn't care. He wouldn't be licking any woman out who went with other men.

"How long has it been since your last man?" he asked, wanting to taste her.

"Years," she said, moaning.

"How long?"

"Erm, three years maybe a bit longer," she said. They were whispering, but he heard her answer.

Glancing at her pussy he saw her cream had slicked her pubic hair. She didn't wax, but her pubic hair was neatly trimmed. Sliding a finger through her slit he stared at what all of his men had wanted to get a look at since her dance.

She was red, puffy, and perfect. He'd never seen such a pretty cunt in all of his life, and he'd seen a fair few to last him a lifetime. Opening her lips he saw her clit peeking out and swollen.

"No men at all."

"Why would I want a man? They're a waste of time."

Her words told him all he needed to hear. The men she'd been with didn't have the first clue in how to take care of a woman. Devil made it his life's work to give a woman pleasure. By the time he was through with Lexie she wouldn't be able to look at another man without thinking of what he could give her first. Devil liked the thought of owning her completely. No woman made him feel this way, and they barely knew each other.

She was a stripper, and he was a biker. Both of them came from the same world but were miles apart from one another.

"Oh, baby. I'm going to show you how wrong you are." He flicked his tongue along her slit, looking up her body to see her cry out.

The noise would wake the boy up, and Devil didn't want to have to stop because of a kid. Lifting a hand between them, he covered her mouth with his palm, muffling any of the sounds that could come out. She didn't fight him as he sucked her clit into his mouth.

Lexie arched against his touch, screaming into his palm. Her hands were clawed into the furniture while she held on for dear life.

Going down from her clit he plunged into her entrance watching her come apart at the same time.

He tongued her cunt, and his dick throbbed almost as if it had a life of its own and knew where it wanted to go. Devil fisted his cock working the pre-cum out of the tip to coat the head.

His other hand still covered her mouth, and he tongued her sweet cream. She tasted so fucking good. He didn't want to stop tasting her.

When he could handle it no more, he flicked her nub watching her face scrunch up and her body shake with need. He wanted to watch her come apart in his arms.

Suddenly, the sound of Simon interrupted their moment. Lexie tensed, staring up at him.

"What the hell am I doing?" She didn't wait for an answer as she scrambled away from him.

Knowing he wasn't going to be inside her tonight, he collapsed to the sofa, hating children at that moment.

"I think you need to leave." She quickly put her nightwear back on then headed toward the only other room in the poky apartment.

Devil knew he could help Lexie out. Over the years he'd built up a good supply of cash and that didn't even include what he kept in his bank accounts. He paid his taxes, and no one was any the wiser.

"I'm not going anywhere."

"You can't stay here."

"Sweetheart, you're not in any position to tell me what I'm supposed to be doing." He sat back watching her.

"Whatever. We're not having sex. You can count that out of the equation." She left him alone.

We're not having sex yet.

He wouldn't stop until he knew how sweet and tight her cunt really was.

After several minutes passed and he could hear nothing else, he walked into the room to find Lexie lying down in bed.

"What are you doing?" she asked, sitting up.

Walking around to the other side, he climbed in.

"No, you can't sleep here."

Devil didn't say a word. Banding his arm around her waist, he tugged her close. She didn't struggle, and he sent thanks to Simon. If the little guy hadn't been in the room she wouldn't have relented at all.

"I'm sleeping here." He pressed his palm against her pussy. "Stop fighting me. We're not going to be doing anything right now."

He didn't move his hand as she settled beside

him. With Lexie in his arms he tried not to think about how right it felt having her there. The women on the road he'd always kicked out never liking his space invaded by a woman.

"Are you going to take him away from me?" she asked.

"No, I'm not going to." He'd already thought about the future. Until he found Kayla, Lexie was going nowhere. "We'll deal with everything else in the morning. Stop worrying and sleep."

Then he did something that surprised him. He kissed her head, settling down with her in his arms.

Chapter Four

The following morning, Lexie tried not to think about the large biker in her bed. She'd woken at seven o'clock after only a few hours of sleep. Making herself a coffee, she sat on the sofa feeding the baby taking sips of her drink every few minutes. All the time she couldn't stop thinking about Devil and his touch on her body.

How can he make me feel this way?

Running a hand over her face she tried to get her rioting emotions under control. Nothing was happening at all. He'd started a fire within her, and she couldn't stop it. Once she finished feeding Simon, she cleaned away her cup only to be started by banging on the door.

She walked toward the door. "Who is it?" she asked.

"Curse."

Recognizing the name, she opened the door. They had ruined what little lock she had last night. He stood looking as threatening as Devil. He was with two other men, and they walked into the apartment looking her up and down.

Their gazes made her blush. She hated thinking of them getting horny over her. Lexie hated the attention and would prefer not to know it was because they'd seen her naked.

"Back off. She's taken," Devil said, walking out of the bedroom. He was completely naked. Gasping, she turned away from him to look at the sink. Didn't he have any problem being naked?

"Look at Boss getting all possessive," Curse said, laughing.

"Shut it. What do you need to tell me?"

She turned back to look at Devil, who was doing up his jeans.

"Boys can't stay at the strip club. Place is a fucking mess, and Vincent is going crazy. We can't open for business tonight, and the guys aren't helping."

"Ripper, stop eyeing up my woman," Devil said. She looked at the red headed man who was staring at her.

Averting her gaze she looked over at Devil.

"Get dressed and start packing up your shit," he said.

"Hell no. I'm not moving into a strip club." She also wasn't allowing herself to be alone with him again.

"You work at the club."

"Doesn't mean I have to live there." She ignored the other guys who were chuckling. Devil stopped her from picking up Simon, and she went to her room alone.

Ignoring Devil and his men, she quickly changed into a pair of jeans and long vest shirt. She tied a sweater around her waist before going to the hole in the wall she called a wardrobe. Pushing her clothes back she opened the little bag that held Kayla's number.

Grabbing her cell phone, which she only used in case of emergencies, she sat on the bed and dialed the number. For the last three months the number hadn't worked.

"Who are you calling?" Devil asked, appearing in the doorway.

Lie. Lie. Lie.

Lying never got her anywhere. Showing him the card, she let out a sigh. "Kayla gave me this number to get in touch with her."

"Why didn't you tell me this last night?" he asked.

"It hasn't worked in the last three months. This is all I have of hers."

"When was the last time you spoke to her?"

"About a month after she dropped Simon off. She

told me she'd be a little longer and to use the money in the envelope. Is that money yours?" she asked.

"Yep, she stole it from me while I was busy."

She nodded. "Look, I don't want to get involved in club business or whatever business you've got going on. I'm not part of this at all."

All Lexie had wanted was a quiet life where she could have a family with no worries and no fears.

"Not going to happen, baby. Kayla made sure of that when she gave you my kid. I've been wrong before, but I got the hunch you can't just walk away from him, can you?" Devil asked, moving to the bed to sit down.

Glancing through the doorway she saw Curse and Ripper playing with the boy.

They looked up and gave her a little wave. Stepping away she walked in front of Devil.

"No, I can't walk away from him. It's like he's my own."

"And he's my first kid. No joke, so don't fucking say anything." He took hold of her hand, turning her palm up. He traced along the crease frowning.

"I don't joke about shit. I don't want to get caught up in this."

"Too late for you. I need you to take care of Simon."

"We're not sleeping in a strip club. I'd rather stay here."

Was she really agreeing to Devil? Crap, there was nothing else she could do but agree with him.

"Vincent called. He's found a place, and we're going to check it out. Boys are organizing a van and car seat. Get your shit packed, and I'm not going to ask again." He tugged her close, and she stumbled against him. Devil was the one in control. There was no hope of her fighting. He wasn't hurting either of them.

His palm pressed against her pussy. The only thing separating them was the fabric of her jeans and panties.

"I'm going to have this, Lexie. Your pussy, your mouth, your ass, the whole of your body is mine."

"You're crazy."

"No, I'm not crazy. I'm determined."

"Why? I'm not Kayla. You can have anyone."

He stared at her without breaking contact. "Vincent was right about you. You've got a low opinion of yourself."

Devil lifted her up and held her in front of the doorway.

"What are you doing?" she asked. Her heart was beating wildly in her chest.

"Boys, what do you think of the lovely Lexie?" Devil asked. One of his arms was wrapped around her waist as the other banded across her chest stopping her from going anywhere.

"Don't know if I should answer that, Boss. You've staked your claim, and I love my dick a lot," Curse said.

"I'm with him."

"Boys, Lexie doesn't think she's all that hot or worth my time. What do you think of that?"

She saw their gazes wander up and down her body.

"I'd fuck her if you let me. Out of all the women on stage she was the fucking hottest. Don't know what women have against food, but fuck me, Lexie, you're fucking hot," Curse said.

Ripper stood up, showing her the evidence of his arousal. "Just by looking at you, sweetheart, and remembering you naked last night."

Devil took his seat back on the bed away from the

men.

"See, you're more than worth my time and I've got to say, I can't wait to feel all of you around my dick." He kissed her neck, holding her in place as he sucked on her flesh.

Moaning, she tilted her head to the side giving him better access.

"That's right, baby. You're going to give me everything. I'm going to get my club a place to live, and you're going to be by my side waiting for me."

His hand cupped her breast, pinching the nipple.

Heat flooded her panties as he worked her body easily. His other hand moved between her thighs, stroking her pussy through the denim.

"Tonight, I'm going to have this pussy, and I'm going to know exactly how tight you are." He bit down on her neck, sucking the tender flesh into his mouth.

"Boss, hate to interrupt you but boys are outside waiting. Vincent is there with his woman to take us to the place."

She heard Devil sigh. Seconds later his arms dropped from around her body. "They've got the worst fucking timing in the world. Fine, we're coming."

He helped her onto her feet.

Cupping her face, he tilted her head back to look at him. "Get your shit packed. My boys will be up to help."

Devil left the room seconds later. Ripper entered the room helping her pack. He didn't say a word, but she felt his gaze on her body. She would never get used to that kind of attention away from the club. When she packed the bedroom up she walked into the other room as Carol knocked on the open front door.

"Honey, what's going on? I saw all of those men outside."

"Something has come up. One of those men is Simon's father. He needs me to, erm, to look after the boy until he's ready to take over." The lies poured out of her mouth.

"Is this the man who beat the shit out of Rob and crushed his hand?" Carol asked. "The very one." Devil appeared in the doorway.

"Then you're all right in my book. I've been trying to get Judi away from that rat bastard. Life on the street is too fucking hard for a girl of her age." Carol took a long drag on her cigarette. "You going to treat this girl well?"

It was like she didn't exist.

"Yeah, and Judi, she's with me and the boys as well. Nothing is happening with her. We're going to send her back to school to finish up."

Carol hummed. "Well, I'll be damned. You just might be the savior we need in this beat up shitty little town."

Piston County wasn't a great place to settle down. It wasn't a small town by any means and had a large upscale area where the wealthy stayed. There was the shitty, poverty stricken area where she lived and then there was the middle ground. The county was like one big line that had different classes of people all wrapped up in one.

What Lexie always found funny was the fact half of the wealthy men stopped by for a little sex from them.

She'd seen plenty of faces in Naked Fantasies. There was enough ground for Chaos Bleeds and the pimps to stay in on the action. Some of the city runaways ended up becoming part of the statistics with the pimps. Either way, if Devil was staying in town then it wasn't going to be safe for Kayla to return at all.

Do you really think she's coming back?

No, she really didn't.
****

"I'm not here to be a savior. I'm here to make money and have a place to stay," Devil said. He didn't want anyone trying to build him up to be something he most certainly was not. Devil wouldn't be the savior in a story.

"Judi owes you her life. Considering you're not a savior, I think you've already got a fan base." Carol turned back to Lexie. "Stay in touch, honey. I love to see you getting out of here."

Carol tapped Devil on the shoulder before leaving.

"Pack your shit up. We've not got a lot of time." Devil helped Lexie pack. Several men walked into the small apartment carrying out everything she owned.

She didn't own all that much. He didn't bother with the sofa or the few pieces of furniture that looked from another century. Kayla had a lot to answer for, along with Lexie's fucking parents. He hated the thought of her struggling to get by.

Every now and then he found himself watching her move around. Her body caught his attention, and he couldn't *not* look at her. He also noticed his men were watching her as well. When she'd been leaning over for ten minutes at a time she stood straight, pressing a hand against her back as she pushed her chest out. The sight made his mouth water, and he knew he was going to make her dance naked for him. Once she finished her dance he'd sink into her tight cunt and never leave her alone.

He'd never felt anything like this before. How had he gone all of his life without craving a woman's touch? Devil loved to fuck women. Over the years he'd left quite a reputation up and down the state.

Walking toward his woman, he wrapped a hand around her neck, drawing her back against him. She gasped, and he covered her mouth with his own.

"The men want to see you naked. You've got them all rock hard for a chance to be inside you."

She pulled away, glancing around the room. His men looked away with noticeable difficulty.

"You're not being fair at all." She turned away, finishing off her packing.

Staring at the rounded curve of her ass, he couldn't resist. Slapping his hand across the rounded cheek, he loved the sound of her cry.

"Mine, remember that."

He carried the boxes down to the van. Phoebe was putting the car seat in the back of the car. Vincent was smoking a cigarette against the car.

"Are you almost done? The agent will be ready within the hour."

"I'm almost ready."

"So you're going to do this, Nick? Become the daddy and be around for your friends?" Phoebe asked, climbing out of the car. She pushed some hair off her face. He watched her slide a hand between Vincent's, rubbing against him.

Nick Dawes was his real name. He hadn't heard it in so long.

"I'm going to give it a try."

"I heard it was because of Tiny." She popped some gum, smiling at him.

Glancing at Vincent, he glared. "Tiny has a set-up. It's working for him, and I'm getting tired of being on the open road."

Phoebe looked over his shoulder. "Now I know why you're giving it ago. Men, always thinking with your dicks."

She left their side.

Looking at where she was going he saw Lexie struggling with the boy and several bags. Phoebe helped taking a bag from her shoulder. Ripper was behind Lexie, grabbing the other bag from her. He saw the interest in Ripper's eyes. It would be all right as soon as they settled down.

Devil hadn't claimed a woman, not even Kayla, for his own. His men would see a whole other side of him once he did.

"Thank you for this," Lexie said, talking to Phoebe.

"Honey, I've got kids of my own. Believe it when I say they need a lot of care, they need a lot of care." Phoebe moved to the trunk of the car.

"Baby, Devil's sitting up front with me."

Phoebe rolled her eyes. "You've only been in town a day, and you're already taking my place."

"I'll never be on my knees sucking your man's cock," Devil said.

He saw Lexie was ignoring him. The lack of response from her irritated him.

Once she'd placed Simon in the car seat, he tugged her out of the car, pressing her against it.

"What are you doing?" she asked.

"You keep asking me that. It's time for you to stop asking questions." Slamming his lips down on hers for all to see, Devil claimed her. He reached down, gripping her ass, and drawing her leg up over his hip. Rubbing his cock against her covered core, he let the whole world see who she belonged to.

Drawing away, he kissed her nose.

Her cheeks were flushed, and a quick glance down showed her arousal.

"Don't worry, baby. I'll have you naked and

begging me in no time."

"Fucking asshole." He heard her mutter the words as she climbed into the car.

Phoebe dropped her sunglasses onto her nose. "Possessive much?"

"Jealous?" he asked, smirking.

"Not on your life. I've got my own man to keep me satisfied."

He really did love Phoebe. She was one of those women you just loved. She didn't judge anyone at all. Her entire being was aimed toward helping others. Vincent had picked himself a keeper.

"Keep telling yourself that."

"I will, Nick. I will."

Devil rolled his eyes as she climbed in the passenger side. Lexie sat behind him with Simon in the middle and Phoebe beside her.

"Your boys following me?" Vincent asked, starting up the car.

"Yeah, I've got a feeling about this place."

"Seriously, you're going to spend money on a feeling?" Phoebe asked.

"I took your man in with a feeling, honey. It's all I've got."

He glanced down at his phone, waiting for the call from Tiny. Snitch being alive was the last thing he wanted to deal with. He knew The Skulls had the first of two drugs runs in the coming week.

Shrugging his shoulders, he pocketed his cell phone.

"You got lucky with my man, Nick."

"Who's Nick?" Lexie asked, speaking up.

"Asshole in the front." Phoebe gave her the answer.

"Your name's Nick?"

"Yeah but I go by Devil. Only annoying bitches call me Nick."

Phoebe burst out laughing, and Vincent along with her. "Don't worry about it, honey. I've learned Devil is all bark and no bite."

Lexie wouldn't be thinking that once he got hold of her. He intended to bite her a whole hell of a lot. Every inch of her skin would know his touch.

"Anything happen on the road?" Vincent asked.

"Nope, not a thing. Got a call from Tiny about something." The boys knew about his past in Fort Wills. The women he'd fucked, all of them willing. He wasn't a fucking rapist no matter what Snitch tried to make him become. Tiny didn't know the real truth of a moment himself.

The bastard held a gun to his head to try to get him to fuck a girl tied up. He didn't know what Snitch's deal was, but it was the first day Devil could have killed the other man. With the gun pressed against his temple, he'd reacted, grabbing his own gun and pointing it at Snitch.

He remembered the words that crossed between them as if it happened yesterday rather than over twenty years ago.

"You will fuck this bitch and show me your loyalty, or I'll blow your fucking brains out."

Devil saw the woman struggling against the arms that held her down. The barrel of the gun pressed against his temple showed him Snitch meant business. With speed that surprised even him, he held his own gun to Snitch's face.

"You think you're a big man, Devil?" Snitch asked, spitting at him.

"No, but I'm a man with nothing to lose. Tell me, Snitch, are you afraid to die?" He cocked his gun ready

to meet death that day.

Pulling out of his thoughts, he glanced behind him seeing Lexie stare out of the window. She was totally innocent. The blonde wig she wore didn't do her justice at all.

"You think you can stick around here?" Vincent asked. "Boys are missing their Uncle Devil."

Laughing, Devil turned back to look out of the front of the car. "Yeah, I'm sticking around for a long time."

The more he thought about settling down the more he liked it. Pulling down his visor he looked at Lexie, who was talking with Phoebe. He'd got more of a reason to stick around.

"You ever heard of a pimp known as Rob?" Devil asked.

Vincent cursed. "Bastard came around to the club over a year ago. You'd left by then, and he demanded his cut. I fucked him up and told him if he ever came around again I'd feed him his balls."

"I caught up with him last night. He's got girls who are not even legal. I stopped him killing a girl last night. She's under my protection, and I want to her set up to head back to school. Scum like this around here a lot?" Devil asked.

If Tiny could clean up Fort Wills with his strict rules then Devil could have Piston County scrubbed up in no time. He didn't have many rules at all, but the ones he did have the men abided by.

"Yeah, some real bad sorts but Rob is the worst. He only deals in kids. I think it's because he can scare them. Takes them away from their parents and all that shit. I don't know how he does it. Bastard or anyone like him comes near my kids he'll be fucking dead," Vincent said.

"That's why I love you, baby." Phoebe tapped him on the shoulder. "You've gotta love a man who'll take care of his family."

Looking at Lexie, he saw her smile.

No one would be hurting her at all. He laid his claim, and all it would take was a matter of time to get a ring on her finger. She would be his. Her fate had been sealed the moment Kayla handed his kid to her.

Chapter Five

With Phoebe holding Simon, Lexie was able to rest her arms as Devil led her around the building. The agent tried to get his attention talking about the benefits of owning the property. He tugged her from one room to the other. Each time he stopped she saw him looking at each corner, assessing and working on to the next.

The boys were downstairs in the main room.

"What do you think?" he asked.

"Why are you asking me?"

"You'll be staying here with me at least until I find a place of my own." He shut the door on the agent, tugging her into his arms. There was nowhere else for her to go. "What do you think?"

"I think you should ask your men. They'd know the answer."

She heard him sigh. Looking up, his gaze kept her on the spot.

"You're going to be difficult about everything, aren't you?"

"It's not my business what you do with your money or where you stay." She held onto his arms afraid he'd let go. Her body was all for him being near her while her mind was torn in two. There was no way it could be possible to feel this way for a man after only just finding out his first name.

"You're still deluding yourself."

"What do you mean?" she asked, dropping her gaze to his lips. She knew what kind of pleasure those lips could create. They didn't get a chance to finish what they started last night. The urge to cross her legs was strong, but she pushed it aside. No, she wouldn't be giving in to that need. She refused to melt like so many other women before her.

"You're under some illusion that you're a free woman." One of his hands went to her neck, pressing his palm to her chest. The other held her still against his body. He was so tall, and she had to pull back a little just to look him in the eye.

"What are you talking about?" she asked.

"The moment Kayla gave you my kid, you became mine. He recognizes you, and if you're the type of woman to walk away from him then you've got me fucking fooled." Devil moved her backwards until the wall stopped her. There was nowhere for her to go. He held her tightly against him.

She shouldn't have liked the way his hand held onto her neck, but she did. Was she losing her mind to fall for man who was so fucking dangerous? Crap, she wanted him so badly. Lexie wished she'd worn a skirt. They could have been fucking right that second and gotten over this burning.

"You feel it, don't you?"

At twenty-one years old she shouldn't be finding Devil attractive. He was old enough to be her father, and yet the feelings inspired inside her were anything but fatherly.

"No, I don't feel anything."

She gasped as his hand slid inside her jeans. Buying a size bigger wasn't the cleverest thing she'd ever done. He found the evidence of her arousal.

"Now, I know what this means." Down his hands went until a finger slid deep into her core. "Tell me what it means, baby."

Lexie shook her head. She refused to give in to him.

A second finger slid inside her with ease. She winced at the tight feel of him inside her. She hadn't been lying when she told him how long it had been.

Having sex had never been enjoyable to her. She knew Devil was going to knock all of her thoughts about sex out of the water.

Licking her lips, she looked up at him.

"How about this?" he asked, shushing her as a third finger was pressed deep into her cunt. She tried to close her legs, but he held her open easily with his booted feet. The man was too strong to stop her.

Don't want to stop him.

"A little tight for you, baby?" His three fingers pumped inside her. "Are you desperate to come?"

Still she ignored him, not wanting to admit to what she needed.

"Last night you left before I could give you what your body so clearly needs." The three fingers he'd been using inside her, he pulled up to stroke her clit.

She cried out, gripping his arm tightly. All of her focus went out of the window.

"Tell me what you want, Lexie. I can give you the world, and all I ask for from you is the truth."

Biting down on her lip she tried to fight her reaction to him. The more he stroked, the harder it was to deny him.

He leaned down, claiming her lips. Devil sucked her bottom lip into his mouth before plunging his tongue inside.

Shattering around his ministrations, Lexie knew she couldn't fight with him. Devil knew exactly what buttons to touch to make her his.

He caressed her clit through her orgasm. All the time she held onto him. It was her second real orgasm, and it shattered her whole world.

Suddenly, she felt the need for a man, a proper man. Her boyfriend had been a selfish prick only interested in his own pleasure and need. She wanted more, a hell of a lot more.

When she could stand the feeling no longer, she gripped his hand, stopping him from giving her anymore.

Taking several deep breaths, she kept her gaze on his.

"You're right," she said.

"About what?"

Gritting her teeth, she held back from slapping him around the face. "I want you."

"That's not good enough."

"What exactly do you want from me?" she asked, raising her voice and losing her temper.

The fingers against her clit moved back down, sliding in deep. She cried out at the fullness. Lexie also felt her cum leaking out. She'd never been so wet before.

"How about you tell me how much you want my dick inside you? I want you, Lexie. I want you on your fucking knees sucking my dick. I want to control how deep you go with my fingers in your hair." The hand around her neck moved up, gripping her hair, showing her exactly how he wanted to hold her. "I want to come in your mouth and watch you swallow every fucking drop." His lips were on hers in the next second, plunging his tongue inside.

He was taking over everything.

"I want to bend you over a fucking table for all my boys to see and fuck your pussy. They will know who owns you. I want my fucking brand on your ass for everyone to see."

"I'm not a piece of cattle," she said, whispering the words.

What shocked her the most out of his statement was how turned on she got at what he said. What would it be like to have a whole room of men watching Devil fuck her? To claim her as his own?

Wrong fucking thing to get turned on about.

"Yeah, I feel how you want it, baby. My men would be fucking their fists while I claim you, baby, wishing it was their dick inside you."

"Stop it," she said.

"No. I'm not going to fucking stop it. You're going to realize your place in all of this. You're not going anywhere."

"This is kidnapping." She didn't believe a word she said.

"No. You're free to go at any time, Lexie. But I will tell you this. You walk out of that door, you leave Simon behind, and you don't come fucking back."

Lexie knew he wasn't kidding. She had two choices, stay with him and be with Simon, or leave, remaining alone.

Don't want to leave.

The ugly truth was the fact she wanted Devil more than she wanted anything.

"I don't want to be shared with your men," she said.

He tilted her head back. One of his hands was still sliding in and out of her core. "Did I say anything about sharing? I said I wanted the men to watch me fuck you. They're going to know who you belong to. It's about time you realized it."

Devil claimed her lips, removing his hand from her jeans. The banging on the door finally brought her back into the present. For the last few minutes everything had been blocked out apart from Devil.

She watched him suck his fingers into his mouth. His fingers were shining with her cream. Lexie felt her cheeks heat up at the sight.

"So fucking tasty." Once he was finished, he took hold of her hand and went to the door. "What the fuck do you want?" Devil asked. The agent looked taken aback.

Keeping her gaze on the nearest wall, Lexie thought about how quickly her life had changed. There really was no going back at all.

****

Devil bought the club and made sure the agent knew he was moving in right away. It wasn't the best place to start with a kid, but it certainly was better than the fucking strip club. Vincent helped him move what little Lexie owned into the club. This place was going to tide him and Lexie over until he found them a house. He liked the thought of going to the wealthy area of town and buying one of the biggest houses in the estate. Devil loved to wind people up. He could just see them now in their pressed suits on their way to work when he walked out with his leathers, heading to the club on his bike.

He'd invested a lot of his money and gotten a good return from the markets. Devil may have spent his years on the road, but it didn't mean he didn't know how to handle his money. The club was what he looked out for nowadays, and nothing was going to change that.

"This place is going to need a lot of cleaning up. I can round up some girls to come and gut this place," Phoebe said, standing beside him.

"That would be great." He looked around the main room and knew he was going to put a bar in along the far wall. There were several tables in different stages of rot. "I can't let Lexie and Simon stay here tonight."

"Our home is always welcome, but you're going to have to be quiet. The boys giggle when you try to fuck."

Devil started laughing.

"We'll be fucking all right. Are you sure you're okay with that?" Devil asked. He tensed as he saw Lexie enter with his son on her hip. She was so fucking

67

beautiful and made his dick ache with need.

They needed to get some time together.

"How about I take Simon for the night and we give you our pool house. The boys will not think to go down there and you'll have you privacy," Phoebe said.

"Did I mention how much I love you?" he asked, kissing her temple.

"Hey, I'm Vincent's, but I know what it's like in those early days. You've got a kid with another woman. The least you can do is give her some loving to butter her up."

"You know I'm not letting her go. Do you think I should?" he asked. Phoebe had put Vincent on the straight and narrow. When Devil hadn't been able to rein his boy in, Phoebe had come along giving him a purpose and a home. Vincent was a good man, but there were times even good men lost their way.

"Nah, she needs someone to take the lead. She's been through too much, and you can see that in her eyes. Vincent was fond of her though. He talked about her all the time. He was impressed with the fact she was taking care of a kid that wasn't actually hers." Phoebe tapped his arms. "Whatever you decide is up to you. I don't think she's going to leave that boy easily, do you?"

She didn't wait for his answer and walked in the opposite direction.

Staring at Lexie he felt like he'd been kicked in the gut. He was old enough to be her father, and yet he was lusting after he like he was some kind of fucking teenager.

"What's up, Boss?" Ripper asked, approaching him.

"Nothing. I'm not sticking around here tonight. You and the boys need to clean that shit up at the strip club. I want it open for business. We need to make our stand. No drugs or squabbles. I don't run a kindergarten," Devil said.

"I'll tell Curse to give the word out."

"You do that."

"Is she sticking around?" Ripper asked, nodding toward Lexie.

"She is, and she's mine. Don't even think about trying to take her. I'll kill you first."

"You're damn lucky. She's sexy as hell, and I bet not many men have been between her thighs."

The thought of any man knowing what she'd be like in bed made him angry.

"Shut it, Ripper."

He left his boys alone to go to Lexie's side. Her hair lay down her back, begging to be held. Standing beside her, he saw she was looking out of the window, pointing things out to Simon.

"We're not staying here tonight."

"Thank God, I thought you didn't have the first clue of the right environment for a baby."

Stroking her hair, he kissed Simon's head.

"He's staying with Phoebe and Vincent. We've got the night in their pool house." Her eyes went wide, but she didn't say anything to dispute him. "Got any questions?" he asked.

"No, you're the boss."

After a couple of hours passed of making a list of things he needed and what would need to happen, Devil left the cleaning in the hands of Phoebe, who had already assembled a team. The ride back to Vincent's house was slow.

Phoebe and Lexie made dinner while he played ball with Vincent and the boys. When the boys started fighting Vincent started talking.

"You've got a thing for Lexie, haven't you?"

Vincent asked.

"What makes you think that?" Devil caught the ball off his friend and dribbled it down to the hoop, landing a shot right in.

He bowed as the boys squealed in delight.

They took a time out as the boys played, trying to score into the high hoop.

"She's a good girl."

"And a stripper," Devil said.

"She was a stripper to take care of your kid. I can't believe I held that boy and you hadn't even seen him."

Devil tensed. "You did the test to make sure she got the body for dancing?"

"Yeah, like I do with all the girls. I didn't touch her at all."

He couldn't be angry at his man for doing business. "She's not dancing anymore, do you hear me?" Devil asked.

"Yeah, I already got that. She made a lot of money."

"Don't care. We'll find other girls who can make that kind of money." Devil stared at the house wondering what shit Phoebe was saying.

"I'm pleased you're going to do right by her. She deserves it."

"You barely know her. How do you know she wasn't passing him off to others to look after?" he asked.

Vincent chuckled. "She talked about him all the time. It was the only reason she danced. I asked her about it, and she told me if another job came around she'd take it in a heartbeat even if it was cleaning toilets. Girl had it bad for the boy. She'd do anything for him." Vincent sighed. "What happened with you and the sister?"

"She was a woman on the road. Didn't give me

any kind of shit and was offering what I wanted, a quick easy fuck. Condom broke and she was pregnant." Devil shrugged. He couldn't do anything to change what happened. It was just rotten fucking luck the one time the condom broke, the girl got knocked up.

"What are you going to do about the girl?"

"I don't know. She'll turn up, and I'll see if I'm in a forgiving mood."

"Dinner is ready," Lexie said, appearing in the doorway. The boys ran in almost knocking her over in their need to get food.

"Where's your fucking manners?" Vincent asked, charging ahead to ward off his boys.

Lexie giggled then smiled up at him. Devil was struck by how young she was. Reaching out she took his hand, and he drew her to him. "What are you smiling about?" he asked.

"Nothing."

He lifted a brow waiting for her to relent.

"Okay, this is something I've always wanted."

"What do you mean?"

"Don't laugh at me, but I imagined having a house like this and calling my man in for dinner with the kids." She shrugged, and her cheeks were a nice shade of rouge. "Do I sound insane?" she asked.

"No, you sound like a woman with a plan. You never lived in a house then?"

She shook her head. "Mom lived in a little flat, and when she couldn't afford to keep up with the rent we moved into a trailer." She shrugged. "There wasn't a lot going on growing up."

Pushing her hair back, he saw the bruises from his lips. "It's good to have dreams."

He was going to make her dreams come true.

"You're not going to tease me?"

"No, I'm going to tell you to hold onto those dreams. They might come true." He leaned down, claiming her lips.

"What are you? My guardian angel?" she asked, between kisses.

"There's nothing angelic about me, baby. Don't mistake me for anything good." Taking her hand, he pressed it to his cock. "All I ever want to be is bad." Rubbing against her, he felt her shudder.

"Kids, dinner is going cold," Phoebe said, interrupting their moment. He was getting fucking angry with people stopping him from taking what he wanted.

Lexie broke away from him. She surprised him by leading him to the dinner table.

"Your woman has got skills," Phoebe said. "She knows how to cook, and you got lucky."

Chapter Six

After dinner, Lexie helped with the dishes, and then there was no getting away from it. Phoebe was pretty much pushing her out of the back door. Devil stood by the pool smoking a cigarette looking up at the sky.

Clearing her throat, she watched him turn toward her. "I'm going to go shower."

"Okay, I'll be in soon."

She nodded, heading past him to go into the pool house. Lexie wasn't stupid. She knew what was coming, and part of her was really looking forward to it. Would he grow bored with her once he got what he wanted?

Glancing back she saw him talking with Vincent. The two men were in a deep conversation with one another. Opening the door, she let herself inside flicking the light on. Phoebe told her where to reach out. The pool house was nice and warm. Grabbing a cable she pulled, and the air conditioning started up. She gazed around the large room before heading toward the back where the bedroom and en-suite bathroom lay.

Closing the door, she flicked the lock in place wanting privacy. For three years and a couple of months she hadn't had sex. The boy she'd been with couldn't even figure out how to give her an orgasm.

Lexie turned on the shower and removed her clothes before staring in the mirror at her reflection. Her hair was limp from the day of moving her stuff, but what caught her attention were her eyes.

Last night she'd stared into the same eyes at the strip clubs mirror, and already there was a difference. Twenty-four hours ago they'd been dead to what she was about to do whereas now they looked alive. She suddenly felt twenty-one instead of much older. Living the life she did with a drunk and whore of a mother, Lexie had learned to grow up really fast. By eight years old she'd been fending for herself in the kitchen, cooking for her small family. Kayla had been out, goading the boys, and when she became a teenager the real action happened. Her sister got the horrid reputation of being a slut. Lexie would always remember the crude whispers as she passed people in school. Some of the guys even thought her mother was better than Kayla because at least her mother made the men pay. Kayla gave everything away for free.

For so long she'd been dealing with everything life threw her way she hadn't the time to think about what she ever wanted. Getting out of the trailer into an apartment had been the first thing she achieved. Not becoming a whore, the second.

Crap, she really didn't know what she wanted out of life. Her grades at school had been good but not brilliant.

She needed to take this time with Devil to think.

The only thing she ever really wanted was to give Simon a really good home.

"He's safe now." Closing her eyes she counted to ten before opening them. Everything looked the same, but she moved toward the shower. The water was hot and made a nice refreshing change from the cold showers she took back at the apartment.

She tried not to think about Devil, the club, or the shit Kayla had put her through. Her sister had never been one to make good decisions. Was having Simon and being with Devil really a bad decision?

Tilting her head back, she kept her eyes closed as the water washed over her body. Slowly, minute by minute she felt the tension inside her begin to ebb away.

We're safe.

"You think a locked door will keep me away?" Devil asked. She'd been so lost in her thoughts she hadn't heard him enter or strip down. Jerking around she saw him butt ass naked. The night before her apartment had been too dark for her to admire his male physique, but damn, Devil was fucking built.

An answering pulse started between her thighs. Crossing her legs she stared up at him, knowing in her heart they were not going to be interrupted.

"We can do tonight one of two ways," he said, trapping her against the cool tiled wall and his hard body. His hands rested either side of her head. Before he said anything else, he took possession of her lips, plunging his tongue into her mouth. She was under no illusions as to who owned her in those precious seconds. "You can fight me, pretending you don't want this and forcing me to show you that you do." He took one of her hands within his own, pressing it against the tile beside her head. Devil did the same with the other hand.

"What's the other option?" she asked.

The way he held her hands had her breasts arching up. His gaze dropped down, and the lust intensified in his eyes.

"You stop pretending and give yourself to me without question. You'll be mine, and I'll give you plenty more orgasms where that first one came from today."

She stared up at him wanting more than anything to give in to him. Licking her lips, she battled a tiny little war inside against her man. Lexie knew it was useless. Why fight something she wanted? Her only sexual experience was with a high school kid her own age, and that had been a disaster.

"What's it going to be, princess?" he asked.

Neither of them said a word.

"Not going to say anything, huh? Fine, let me give you a little taste of what I'm offering." Her hands were lifted above her head, and he caught them within one of his. She didn't fight him. The strength in his arms let her know fighting would be futile. "This what you want, baby?" he asked, leaning down to kiss her chest.

Words failed her. They wouldn't come out of her mouth, and she watched him, filled with desire as he kissed down to her breasts. He sucked a nipple into his mouth, and all the time she watched even as she cried out in pleasure.

The hand he had free, caressed up her inner thigh. The water cascaded around them, the droplets bouncing off their skin. Even wet, Devil looked like a fucking wet dream. This was pure torture. Every move, each caress, and all the words he spoke drove her arousal higher than she ever thought it could be.

"What do you hope to gain by being silent?" he asked. His fingers were so close to her pussy. Biting her lip, she looked him in the eye waiting for him to make the next move. "You're playing with danger here, baby."

She wanted the danger more than anything else.

What the hell is wrong with me?

"I can play this game all day, Lexie. You're not hiding anything from me."

Fingers opened her slit, stroking through until he bumped her clit. She cried out as Devil increased the pressure around her wrists, holding her in place. Down his caress went to push a finger inside her. His thumb pressed against her clit.

"I can feel your cunt tighten around my finger. You want my dick, Lex. I promise you, I'm a lot bigger than my fucking finger."

Closing her eyes, she tried to fight against the need flowing within her body.

"Give in to me."

She opened her eyes and stared into his dark depths.

"Give in to me," he said, again.

Give in. Give in.

What exactly was she fighting? She wanted him, and for so long she'd been without ever knowing what true passion really was. The experience she had when she was younger wouldn't be anything like what Devil was offering her.

A second finger slid inside her joining the first, pumping in time. He bit down on her nipple drawing a scream from her.

"Give in to me, Lex. I will give you everything."

She'd already given in. Lexie was no longer fighting him. Her body had betrayed her the first night he held her in the strip club. This was going to happen, and fighting it would only cause her more ache.

Her body was burning from the inside out.

There was nowhere else for her to go. At twenty-one years old she had experienced two orgasms in her whole life, and both had been at Devil's hands.

He slammed his lips down on hers stopping her from saying a word. His tongue plundered her mouth, melding with hers.

She melted against him, his body covering hers.

"Tell me, Lex."

Looking down his body she was caught by his muscles and the large displays of ink up and down his body. She hadn't even taken into account the many different tattoos when he'd walked into the shower.

"You're older than I am," she said, the words blurting out.

"Do you really care?" he asked.

No, she did not. "No."

"You want me."

"Yes," she said, admitting the truth. She really did want him. There was no denying it.

"Tell me to fuck you. I promise you, Lex, you'll want for nothing.

"Fuck me, Devil."

She gave in to him, and he released her hands.

"Good, first we're going to get washed, and then your ass is mine."

****

Devil finished washing the soap out of her hair. Lexie had remained silent as he washed her body. She didn't fight him, but she kept staring at him as he worked. When he was done, he turned the water off and handed her a towel. Wrapping a towel around his waist, he walked into the bedroom waiting for her to follow. Sitting down, he dried his hair as she walked into the room. Her hair was semi-dry as she bunched the length up with a towel.

"Come here," he said.

She walked over to him. He saw the hesitation in her eyes as she stood between his thighs. His dick thickened, and he knew he wouldn't last the first time he was inside her.

Tugging on the towel, he watched it fall to the floor. Her body was damp.

Reaching around, he brought her closer with a grip on her ass. He pressed kisses along her stomach, watching her close her eyes.

"Have you ever felt like this before?" he asked. Her stomach was visibly quivering as she gazed down at him. Her eyes looked almost black with the dilation of her arousal.

"No, never."

"How many men have you fucked?" Opening her

legs, he scented her arousal.

"One."

"Over three years ago?" Covering her mound, he felt her cream leak onto his fingers. She was so fucking wet for him.

"Yes. He was my first boyfriend and didn't have a clue what to do."

He smiled. "Climbed on and rode his way for his own release?" Devil knew the sort. Some men really didn't know how to awaken a woman sexually. He learned from a young age that to get the woman he wanted in bed he first needed to spend the time working her up into a frenzied need. Devil also liked an open woman in the bedroom. He couldn't be done with a woman scared to want to fuck. There was no time for him to draw a woman unwilling to give herself to him. He didn't do unwilling women who fought everything straight away.

Lexie wanted him, and she was only fighting her need. Now, he saw she was giving herself to him.

"Yeah, he was a real piece of work. I didn't like him at all, and we parted ways a while ago."

Good, he would have to beat the shit out of anyone who tried to make a claim on her.

"Straddle me."

She climbed onto his lap, wrapping her legs around his waist. He claimed her lips, tasting her as her body rode his. Her naked tits pressed against his chest, and they were real.

Turning her, he slid between her legs as she kissed him back. The bed sheets were wrinkled underneath them. The towel he had on slipped off, and he slid his cock between her slit. Her cream coated his shaft. In no rush, he bumped her clit feeling her relax beneath him.

When he could take the feel of her slit no longer, he broke the kiss working down to suck on her nipples. She arched under him. Gripping her hips, down he went, sliding a tongue into her belly button before going down. Opening her thighs wide he stared at her puffy, red slit. Using his thumbs he opened the lips of her sex to reveal her swollen clit and the entrance to her cunt.

Closing the distance he sucked her clit into his mouth, much like he'd done with her nipples. Flicking his tongue over her nub, he glided down to fuck her pussy. She cried out. Glancing up, he saw her back arch off the bed.

"Please, yes, please," she said, moaning.

He loved hearing the sounds of her begging. Going back up, he tongued her clit wanting her to orgasm before he slammed deep inside her.

She gasped, and still he kept up his ministrations wanting her to come apart. His cock was so fucking hard it hurt.

It had been too fucking long since he'd fucked a woman. Lexie was driving him crazy, and he knew if he didn't get inside her soon he'd be suffering with blue balls.

"Come for me," he said, muttering the words against her clit.

Sliding a finger inside her, he tongued her clit.

Seconds later she screamed out in climax. Smiling, he continued caressing her clit as she screamed, shuddered, and jerked underneath his touch. Only when he was satisfied did he pull away, wiping her cum from his lips and face.

"I'm clean, are you?" he asked.

"Yes, but I'm not protected," she said, breathlessly. He cursed. Climbing off the bed, he grabbed a condom from the drawer, quickly tearing into the foil to cover his cock with the latex.

Lexie stayed in the same place. He moved between her thighs, sliding his covered cock through her slit. It wasn't good enough, but until she was on the pill he'd have to use rubbers. He wasn't ready to give her a kid yet. When he was ready there was going to be no stopping him in what he wanted to give her.

"Are you ready for this?" he asked.

"Yes."

Pushing the tip inside her cunt, he gripped her hips and slammed inside. She cried out. Her pussy was so fucking tight. Groaning, he rested his head against hers as she grew accustomed to him inside her.

"You're, erm, you're a little big."

He chuckled.

"Baby, you know what to say to make a man crave you." Kissing her lips, he gave her a couple of minutes before pulling out of her tight heat only to thrust back inside. The sudden jolt made her tits bounce. Rearing back, he watched her tits as he thrust inside her, feeling her tight heat surround him.

The sight alone made his balls tighten. Gritting his teeth, he closed his eyes as the pleasure intensified. He stilled within her. If he moved Devil knew he wouldn't last. He was so close to the edge of orgasm. The control he had could only last so much before he blew apart. There was no way he was only going to be like the other man in her life.

He'd been fucking for a lot longer and knew what to do to bring his excitement down. Her body was addictive. It was hard for him not to pound away until he came.

Running his hands up her body, he cupped her breasts pinching her nipples. "Why have you stopped?" she asked.

"I'm not ready to call an end to it." Biting down on her nipples, he moved her legs to circle his waist.

In one quick movement he pulled her up, turned until she was on top with him sitting up. Her arms banded around his neck, holding onto him.

Gripping her ass he brought her up and down on his shaft. She moaned, moving her hips in time with each of his thrusts.

"You're so fucking sexy," he said. Reaching in front of them, he fingered her clit, watching her cry out, begging for more. "Come for me, baby."

"I can't," she said.

"Yes, you can, and I'm not coming until you give me what I fucking want." He slammed inside her, going deeper, and she cried out. The look on her face was a cross between pleasure and pain. "This is only the beginning, Lex. We've got all night and the rest of our lives."

She gasped. Her pussy tightened further around his cock.

"I can't."

"Give me your cum." Caressing her clit he knew it was only a matter of seconds before she climaxed. Her hands tightened on his shoulders. Her breathing got deeper, and he added a second finger to stroke her clit. She was shaking and her whole body covered in a layer of perspiration.

"Come on, baby. Give it to me."

She screamed out, and he took possession of her lips at the same time as slamming inside her. Two thrusts was all it took to find his climax. Growling out, he held her to him, biting on her flesh as the pleasure rode him hard.

He knew without the condom he'd feel every ripple and the wash of her cum. Devil needed to get her on the pill so he could get what he wanted.

"Devil," she said, moaning.

They came down together, and he stroked her hair, loving the feel of the silky strands wrapped around them. Her hair was long, brushing the top of her buttocks. Kissing her lips, he pulled his hand away and then licked her cream off his fingers.

She tasted so sweet.

"You really are the devil."

He chuckled. "If I'm the devil, what does that make you?" he asked.

"I don't know. I can't believe I'm doing this."

"Why not?" he asked, feeling her pussy still rippling around him. She whimpered.

"I don't know you at all. Nothing makes any sense when I'm around you." Her fingers were stroking circles in his flesh.

"Don't give a fuck how long we've known each other. You want to be here with me, then fucking be here with me. Don't over-analyze everything. You'll waste your life away trying to act like others think you should."

Gripping her ass, he tightened his hands around her plump flesh. Her body really was a fucking dream.

"So I should stop fighting what I know?" she asked, smiling.

"Yeah, I'm not going to grade you on good behavior, princess."

"What will you grade me on?"

She was teasing him.

He laughed, loving the sudden change inside her. "I'll grade you on being so fucking bad."

Chapter Seven

A little after midnight Devil carried her, naked, out to the swimming pool. The pool was obscured from the main house so no one would see them swimming. She stared up at him as he stood on the edge of the pool about to climb in. The ink stood out against his tanned flesh.

"You know, for an old guy, you're ripped," she said, smiling.

"Old guy?" he asked, raising a brow. "Did I feel old to you in there?"

She couldn't believe the stamina of the man. After their first time she thought that would be the end of it, sleep, then wake up in the morning. Not Devil. After he removed the condom and threw it in the trash, he had a smoke, and then he was on top of her again. She couldn't complain. He always made sure she found release before he found his.

"Do I look like I care?" she asked, standing up in the water to show off her breasts. She padded to the side of the pool. He sat down on the edge, and she stroked his length. "Are you coming inside?"

"I like this side of you," he said. She worked his length, feeling him thicken in her palm.

"You do?" Using his legs for leverage, she kissed his lips.

He kissed her back and she moved away from him in the pool. "So, what was Kayla to you?" he asked, climbing into the water. The sudden change of subject surprised her. Swimming around the edge of the pool she thought about her sister.

"We're half-sisters. She came first and me a few years later." She turned, watching him in the water. He wasn't advancing toward her, and she stopped swimming to look at him.

Even in the low lighting of the pool, he looked so big and terrifying. He didn't scare her at all. No, he made her ache.

"Were you close?" he asked.

"No. Our mom liked her a lot more than me because she was blonde, beautiful, and perfect. At least, by our mother's standards, she was perfect." Lexie pushed the hair out of her face, staring at him. "She used to thieve off everyone. No one would suspect the crying blonde girl of taking shit. Mom thought it was funny, and so Kayla stole until boys became her thing."

"What did you do?" he asked.

"I stayed out of the way. There's only so many times you get slapped around the face before you realize you're better out in the dark than at home."

She saw him visibly tense.

"By the time Kayla was a teenager she had more men than you could count on both hands. She loved the attention, and with her looks and figure, she had all the men eating out of her hand. That time was the *only* time that Mom hated her."

"Why?"

"Kayla didn't charge. I was useless. I earned money waitressing or cleaning some of the houses up for rich people."

Neither of them moved. Lexie wondered what the hell was happening between them. "Where did you meet her?" Lexie asked, struck by jealousy.

"On the road. She was in a bar one night looking for some action. I needed some relief. She was there and didn't cause a fuss."

"How did she get to steal over ten thousand dollars?" she asked.

He started walking toward her. Only when he was

a few steps away did she try to swim away. He caught her around the waist, drawing her back against him. His hands were on her stomach, her back to his chest. Devil buried his face against her neck, inhaling her in.

Her body was covered in bruises from his rough possession. The marks didn't make her terrified. The marks made her want him so much more. She craved his rough possession. Her body was aflame for his touch.

"I'm not a good man, Lex. I break the law to make money. The ten thousand dollars was from a drug run for a friend. The money was going into our liquid cash fund that Vincent takes care of. No one looks at cash hidden within a safe." He kissed her neck, breathing her in.

"How come I've never seen you here before?" she asked.

"It has been a long time since I've been here, and I didn't make a lot of fuss. Vincent fell in love with Phoebe, and I wasn't going to screw that up for him when I knew I wasn't sticking around." One of his hands moved up to cup her breast. "Have you been here your whole life?"

"Yes. I've never heard of you."

"I doubt Kayla even knew who I was. Crazy bitch is going to learn not to steal money from me and get away with it." He kissed her neck. "Your sister is as good as dead."

The words shocked her. Turning in his arms she looked him in the eye. "What are you talking about?" she asked.

"No one steals from me. I'm not a fucking charity. She took without even asking. Bitch stole my money and my kid. She will pay."

Her heart was thumping against her chest. "What about me? I took Simon and the money. What are you going to do with me?"

Devil tilted her head back, letting her go. "I'm not going to kill you. What Kayla did was fucking stupid, but she knew I was going to go looking for her. I bet she's hoping you'll take her place, easily."

Lexie wished she could deny it. "You think she wants you to kill me?"

"Kayla's no fucking saint, Lex. She's hoping I'll be so fucking angry I'll take it out on your ass." Devil smiled. "Just goes to show the bitch doesn't know me at all."

"What are you talking about?"

"I don't take debts out on family members who are not involved. My problem with Kayla will be settled with her."

She looked down into the water. Lexie wasn't scared or even upset by his words. She and Kayla had never been close at all. Taking in Simon had been the closest thing to sisterly love that Lexie had ever done. Not that she had much choice. Kayla had simply dumped her kid on her doorstep. Devil's reasoning explained the ten thousand dollars.

"Are you scared of me?" he asked, taking a step closer.

Lexie shook her head. She didn't trust her voice in that instant. How horrible was she that she still desired the man who threatened her sister?

"Good." His arms surrounded her, and he moved her close to the edge of the pool. "Hold on here." He put her hands on the edge.

Gripping the ledge, she wondered what he was going to do. He moved the hair off one shoulder, leaving it to trail down the side. The tender way he touched her surprised her. She had started to believe he didn't know how to be gentle or tender with her.

"Don't let go."

"I won't." The air between them changed. She didn't know what had happened to make it so.

Devil laid his lips against her temple, kissing her. Closing her eyes, she tried not to be drawn into the web of seduction he was creating. The man behind her was dangerous.

Licking her lips, she tried to think past her own arousal. For once she felt selfish as she didn't wish to think about anything else but herself.

"This thing between us," he said. "It's going to last a long time. You better understand what is happening."

"Why don't you tell me? You're not speaking words of love."

"I don't love anyone, baby."

The words didn't hurt, but she knew what he meant by them. There would never be any words of love between them. This was the reality of everything they were doing. What happened when the chemistry fizzled out?

Don't think. Feel.

His lips grazed her neck, nipping at her flesh. Tilting her head to the side she gave him better access. His hands caressed her body, cupping her tits and tweaking the nipples. Still, she held onto the ledge keeping her eyes closed. Everything else faded away. There was only the two of them hidden away in the darkness. The warm air washed over her shoulders, and she shivered as his touch moved down to her pussy. One hand slid down, caressing her slit, stroking her, heightening her arousal for what was about to come.

"I've got you, Lex."

She felt protected. Devil wouldn't let anything happen to her providing she didn't betray him. The club would be like a family to her. The answers she'd been missing for a long time came to her as he touched her body. She knew he was holding himself back. Devil was many men, and this time he showed her another part of himself.

Opening her legs, she cried out as he pressed two fingers inside her. His cock was huge, much bigger than his fingers, yet she felt tender from everything he'd done.

"I'm not asking for love." Seeing what happened on the streets with married men looking for a night of release, Lexie had long given up the dream of ever finding love.

Love was for princesses and fairy tales. She'd stopped believing in fairy tales at a young age. Fairy tales didn't pay the bills or stop bad men from coming in the night.

"You'll be mine," Devil said.

"In what way?" She felt him stroke her body. His cock poised at her entrance.

"You'll be my woman. No other man will touch you. You'll be waiting for me, night after night." He slid inside her, achingly slowly. "You'll never deny me." He bit down onto her neck. The marks were going to stay there forever. "You'll stop stripping and will only strip when I say so."

He gripped her hips, slamming in deep for the last inch. They both cried out. Holding onto the ledge, Lexie opened her eyes. He felt so large behind and inside her. His hands swamped her thick hips.

"All I've got to do is agree?" she asked.

"Yes."

"I thought I agreed back at the club? I didn't walk out of the door."

"You agreed not to leave Simon. You didn't agree to being my woman." He pulled out of her only to slam back inside.

She groaned, loving the depth of every thrust. The mention of Simon brought her back to reality. They were in the pool, and his dick was inside her, his very naked dick was inside her.

"You've got to stop," she said, panicking.

"No."

"You're not wearing anything. I could get pregnant." He paused. Their heavy breathing was the only sounds to be heard in the still night.

"I don't give a fuck." He pulled out of her only to slam back inside, sliding a hand between her slit to play with her nub. All thought of denying him or stopping the sex vanished from her thoughts. By the edge of the pool, she came apart in his arms as he fucked her hard. Nothing was left between them. Devil knew what Kayla had done, and in turn, she had become his woman.

His lips trailed fire down her neck, making her burn even deeper. Devil's thrusts grew erratic, his fingers working her expertly hurtling her toward another orgasm. Seconds after her own, she heard him growl as his cock jerked.

Their fates were already sealed.

****

The following morning, Devil stared at Lexie's body. He'd kept her up to the early hours of the morning, fucking her. Their time in the pool hadn't ceased. Once he'd climaxed, without a rubber, inside her, he'd carried her inside, laid her on the bed and fucked her twice more. From a young age he'd always had a high libido. She hadn't gotten any rest last night at all.

He admired her full curves on display as most of the blanket was off her body.

Her face was turned toward him. She looked so relaxed in sleep. Devil loved looking at her. He recalled the feel of her rounded ass resting against him as he fucked her hard.

Devil ran his hand down the length of her body. She mumbled something, snuggling in the bed.

Lighting up a cigarette, he climbed out of bed to wander out of the bedroom toward the door. He opened up the door to see Vincent on his way down. Grabbing his jacket he placed it over her ass and quickly pulled up his pair of jeans as Vincent came to the door. From the vantage point where Vincent stood he could see into the room. He'd covered up his woman's personals, not ready to share them with anyone. Fucking her in the club for all of his men to watch would be different from sharing her.

"Did you have a good night?" Vincent asked, taking a seat.

"Very. What brings you down here so fucking early?" Devil asked, carrying out to the recycle bin the few bottles of beer they'd drunk.

"Phoebe's dealing with the kids, and I like to stay away from that chaos. She's organizing the cleaning crew for the club. They'll be there in an hour or so to start gutting the place." Vincent leaned back in his chair. "She your old lady?"

"She's my woman. I guess she'll be considered my old lady." Sitting down, Devil inhaled on his cigarette looking at his friend.

"Got word that Rob has been pissing himself about you."

Devil laughed. "What's the news then?" he asked, wanting to take his mind of his woman's naked ass. He had yet to fuck it, but it would only be a matter of time.

"You crushed his hand. He's been trying to rally some of the other pimps and clients in a bid to make life difficult for you."

"Can he do it?" Devil asked.

"His clients are some of the richest people in the county. I doubt they'd try to get their hands dirty with a known pimp. His girls are underage," Vincent said.

"I can't believe this is so fucking bad. How is Judi doing?" Devil asked.

"Curse and the guys have gotten her working at the club. She's cleaning rooms, and Phoebe's looking into getting her back at school. I don't know how she's going to take that, but we'll handle the problem when it arises."

Devil waited for him to continue.

"What are you going to do? Are you going to keep them at the club, or are you actually going to settle down and do what Tiny has done?" Vincent asked.

"I'm settling down. I'll still go on the road, but I'm looking to find a house."

Vincent chuckled, pulling out some paperwork from his jeans pocket. "My woman knows you better than I realize."

He handed over the piece of paper. Devil took it from his fingers, opening up the folded papers. "What is this?"

"A house. It's within the wealthy area. Phoebe knows how you like to piss people off, and she figures this will be big enough for you and Lexie. Also, any of the club who sticks around, and if you see here," Vincent pointed at the garden, "it's big enough for a garden for the barbeques she wants you to throw."

"Your woman has everything planned out, doesn't she?" Devil asked. Phoebe was always prepared, which was one of the things he liked about her.

Looking through the paperwork, he heard Lexie moan. She rolled over in bed and gasped.

"We're out here, baby."

Minutes later she walked into the room wearing a

pair of shorts and a vest. "I found them in the drawer," she said, going to the sink. Lexie smiled at Vincent. "Morning."

"Morning. You don't need to be embarrassed, Lex. I've got no problem with you being here."

"Okay."

Devil looked over the paperwork, knowing he'd need to see the house before he even thought about buying it. "I want to check it out."

"I'll get Phoebe to organize a viewing." Vincent stood and left them alone.

"What was that all about?" Lexie asked. She poured them both a coffee.

"I'll have cream and sugar," he said.

He liked the way she followed his orders adding what he asked for. Devil watched her, liking the domestic feeling she inspired within him. He stayed in one place only going on the necessary runs, and he could have this for the rest of his life. After their time in the pool he'd not even bothered with a condom. They were a waste of time anyway.

Liar, you just like the feel of her naked against you.

"Do you want me to go to the pharmacy today?" she asked, sitting down in Vincent's vacant chair.

"Why?" She wasn't wearing a bra, and he was getting a little distracted by her naked breasts on display that were only covered by a shirt.

"For the morning after pill?"

"No, you don't need it. We'll deal with whatever happens."

"I don't want kids yet," she said, blowing on her coffee.

He knew she was being reasonable while he didn't feel the slightest bit reasonable.

"I'll use rubbers, but you're not taking the morning after pill. That's final." He stood up, going into the bedroom to grab his jacket. "We're going to look at a house today. I'll be up at the main house. Come to me when you're ready."

He left the pool house heading toward the main house. Phoebe was bundling the kids into the car as he approached. She smiled at him. "Where's your other half?"

"Pissing me off. Vincent inside?" he asked.

"Yeah, your viewing is at ten. Be sure to be there. I'm taking Simon for the ride. We'll be back later."

Heading inside he found Vincent going over some paperwork. "What's happening?"

"Nothing, just going through the paperwork for the club. Here, check it out."

Devil took the folder and checked through the numbers. He didn't see anything wrong. "Business is going good?"

"Yeah, my concern at the moment is with Rob. He's a young fucking punk who doesn't know when to bow down." Vincent removed the glasses he'd been wearing.

Thinking about Rob made Devil's anger spike. He had enough of hearing about the fucking bastard who used young girls.

"It's fucking wrong what he's doing," Devil said. "I'll put the bastard in the fucking ground."

"I got a call. Jerry wants to meet with you," Vincent said.

"Who the fuck is Jerry?" Devil was growing tired of all the names. Is this what Tiny had to put up with? He'd only been in town a day and already was on the bad side of a pimp and another wanted a meeting.

"He's a pimp but a fair one. He owns a private

club that is pretty much a whore house."

"What's the difference between this fucker and Rob?" Devil asked.

"Jerry keeps his girls safe. None of them are on the street, and he's one of the big leagues. Owns a house a couple down from the one you're going to view. He's got a wife and a couple kids. A mistress, too." Vincent tapped his hand on the table. "You'd be best meeting with him."

"Fine. You coming with me to view the house?"

"I can if you want me there," Vincent said.

"Yeah, I want you there." The sound of the back door opening drew him up short. "She doesn't need to know what we're going on a meeting about."

Lexie rounded the corner and smiled at them.

Fuck, the smile on her face felt like a fucking kick to the gut. Devil knew he was feeling something a lot more than liking. There was no fucking way he loved Lexie. He didn't do love, and for a long time, he'd cut himself off from all emotion. Having a gun pressed against his head reminded him he needed to keep love at bay.

"Come on, let's go," he said, heading out of the house.

She didn't say anything, simply climbed into the back of the car as he went to view a house.

Three hours later, Devil signed along the dotted line. He loved the look and feel of the place. It was five beds with a pool and plenty of garden space to host a couple of barbeques. His life was moving along.

Glancing down at his cell he saw nothing new from Tiny. It was only going to be a matter of time before his friend got in touch. He felt it in his blood.

Taking Lexie with him to Jerry's house, he saw the bastard was loaded. For the next hour he talked business with the biggest pimp of Piston County. Even though the fucker sold women to make a living Devil couldn't help but like him.

Life was looking interesting. The biggest problem he had was what to do with Lexie. The bitch was getting under his skin, and they'd not known each other all that fucking long.

Chapter Eight

One week later Lexie stood in the kitchen of Devil's new house. Most of his men were stood out in the garden nursing beers as he cooked food at the barbeque. She was amazed at what the man could accomplish in a matter of a week. He'd purchased this luxury house, reorganized building work on his clubhouse, and tidied up the strip club. The man was a machine.

At night he joined her in bed awakening her body in the way only he seemed to know.

"What are you thinking about?" Devil asked, appearing behind her. They were the only two in the kitchen. Glancing toward the barbeque she saw Ripper flipping burgers.

"Nothing much."

"Come on, share them. We've not gotten chance to talk all week." His hand banded around her waist, drawing her back against him.

Judi had moved in with them the same week. Devil wanted her to finish school, and every time Lexie thought she hated the sight of him, he always did something that made her like him a little bit more. The young girl had been forced to grow up too fast. Lexie knew the feeling, but she also knew she hadn't been through what Judi had.

The girl was strong, and looking out at the garden Lexie saw her reading one of the course books that had been sent by the school. Judi needed to pass an exam to get back into school to finish her last two years.

"You're not who I thought you was."

"Baby, don't go getting sentimental on me. I'm fucking dangerous, and the moment you think otherwise, will be your mistake." He turned her around, lifting her up onto the kitchen counter.

His lips slammed down on hers, and she whimpered as his hands roamed her body. "Fuck me, I can't get enough of you."

Without any word to his men, he lifted her in his arms and carried her toward the stairs.

"Boss, food's ready," Curse said.

"Then feed your fucking selves and keep yourselves occupied."

Burying her head against his neck, she groaned at the knowing look in Curse's eyes.

"Have fun."

Groaning, she held on tighter to his neck. "You're not being fair. How can I face them again?"

"With a smile on your face knowing I've fucked you good." He kicked open their door, slamming it behind him. She giggled as he dropped her to the floor.

He tugged out the band holding her hair up.

Next he fingered the length, sinking his hands in and fisting them. She gasped at the bite of pain from the pull of his hands.

His lips covered hers, and her pussy bloomed. She crossed her legs knowing she wanted him badly.

Devil broke from the kiss, releasing her. "You're going to dance for me," he said.

"What?"

She watched him walk toward the stereo, and a slow moving tune filled the air.

"No one else is here. I saw you dance. You didn't want any of the men there. If they had touched you, I know you'd have hated it." He sat down on the edge of the bed.

He removed his leather cut showing his Chaos Bleeds MC status.

"This time I want you to dance for me, knowing

only I am going to be the one to fuck you in the end."

Her heart pounded against her chest. She had never danced for anyone in her life. The music flowed around them.

"Dance for me."

It wasn't a request, but she felt the urge to please him, to have something between them. None of the men were ever going to see her dance again. Nodding her head, she took a step back, turning away from him. She didn't think about money or Simon, only her need to feel his hard dick sliding inside her. They were far enough from the garden that she didn't even hear them talking

You can do this.

She allowed all of her desire and arousal to flow into her movements. First she worked her hips knowing what he loved about her body. The jeans she wore rode low on her hips leaving her slightly rounded stomach on display. The vest shirt was pulled taut over her large breasts. Devil liked to see her curvy figure and wouldn't allow her to wear anything that would obscure his view of her body. Part of her was thrilled with how taken he was of her body. Another part hated being on display.

Years of being told she was fat, ugly, and disgusting could do that. Her mother and Kayla had worn away at her confidence from a young age. Dancing hadn't brought it back, but she was starting to think Devil was determined to.

Turning around, she sank her fingers into her hair and danced, keeping her gaze on his. Devil's gaze travelled up and down her body, landing on her breasts. She really liked the fullness of them, especially when he loved to play with her. For an entire movie she'd sat between his legs as he stroked her breasts.

He drove her crazy while he was just happy to hold what was his.

She unbuttoned her jeans, spinning back to him showing her ass. Lexie heard him groan as she wiggled out of the denim then kicked it aside. She wore a pair of lace panties.

Moving back, she allowed him to touch her ass. Taking hold of his hands, she ran them up and down her body. This was not a dance on stage, and she needed his touch to keep her in place.

When he made to touch her breasts, she stopped him, pulling away and shaking her head.

"This was a bad fucking idea," he said, muttering.

Smiling, she shook her head, dancing toward the next song. Several seconds passed, and she pulled up her shirt, showing him a glimpse of the lace bra she wore. Her nipples would be on full display and easily visible through the sheer fabric.

Glancing down, she saw the clear evidence of his arousal.

She tugged the vest shirt up over her head, hiding her chest from his view.

"Fucking tease," he said.

"This is what you wanted." She pointed out the truth to him. Lexie didn't deserve any teasing at all. She was simply following his orders. He'd not given her much choice.

She couldn't deny the arousal, though, at dancing only for him.

Moving closer, she reached behind her tearing off the bra. She pushed his hands away, cupping her breasts in offering to him.

"Fuck me, you're something else entirely." He flicked his tongue over her nipples, and she cried out at the feel of his tongue on her ultra-sensitive skin.

Arching up, she felt his hands grip her ass rubbing her against his cock. He was thick, hard, and throbbing.

Her desire to do something else had her pulling out of his lap.

"The dance is over."

She sank to her knees, going to the button of his leathers. Together they worked to pull his cock out of the tight confines that bound him. He was long and thick. The tip of his shaft leaked his pre-cum.

Smiling up at him, she licked the tip in the same way he'd licked her nipples.

"Fuck." He cursed, sinking his fingers into her hair as she continued to lick his cum from the tiny slit at the tip. He didn't ram his dick into her mouth. Devil waited patiently for her to take him into her mouth.

His fingers were soothing as she licked along the thick vein pulsing with blood. The song changed, and she ignored it. She stayed knelt on the floor, sucking his cock into her mouth. Taking the tip in first she worked more and more of him inside until she had more than half of his cock.

There was too much for her to take at once. Devil took over, fisting her hair, pulling her off and thrusting back into her mouth. His cock was coated in her saliva, which didn't seem to bother him at all.

She kept her mouth open as he fucked her mouth hard. The thrust were deep but not to the point of making her gag.

Staring up at him, she saw the pleasure shining in his eyes.

"No, I don't want to come in your fucking mouth." He tugged her off his cock and brought her up for a kiss. She moaned as he thrust his tongue into her mouth.

With quick easy moves, he turned her to the bed, putting her on her knees. "This is how I want to spend my days."

Lexie gasped. His fingers probed her pussy, sliding through her slit, coating his digits with her cream before caressing her bud. He knew just how to touch her to get what he wanted.

Closing her eyes, she moaned as his other hand caressed her ass.

In different motions he fingered her pussy at the same time dragging some of her lube back to her anus. She tensed up, but he tapped her clit, making her forget everything else.

"Fuck, I can't wait."

His touch disappeared, and then she screamed as his cock found her entrance and was rammed right to the hilt inside her. There was no way he put a condom on in such a short time. Licking her parched lips, she groaned as his cock seemed to jerk like it had a mind of its own inside her.

Gripping the sheets beneath her body she wondered how on earth she was going to survive his harsh fucking. He had the power to make her melt, and there was nothing she could do to stop his brand of possession.

****

Fuck, he could so get fucking used to this. Closing his eyes, Devil gritted his teeth as he waited for her rippling pussy to cease. The bitch was going to kill him at this rate. Holding onto her hips, he felt her wriggling on his shaft.

"Be still," he said, slapping her ass.

The red of his handprint stood out in contrast to her whole body. Was there nothing this woman did that didn't turn him the fuck on?

The music flowed into the room creating a steady, throbbing beat. Gazing down the length of her back, he found it deeply erotic that she was completely naked while he was fully dressed. His cock stood out through the opening of his slacks, now buried without a rubber in her tight, little cunt. He was going to nickname her special place heaven. Devil sure felt like he was in heaven inside her.

Reaching around, underneath her, he slid his fingers through her creamy slit, coating them with more of her cum. The dance she'd given him had been pure perfection. He loved watching her body move, the thrust of her tits, the sway of her hips—all of it turned him on. There was no way he'd let her dance again. Only he would get the privilege of seeing her dance. The more he thought about what she sacrificed for him the harder it was to pull away. All of those years ago when Snitch had pressed the barrel of a gun to his head, he'd been ready to die. In fact, he'd welcomed it.

Devil knew the only thing that kept him alive had been the fact he had nothing to lose. He really hadn't cared if he lived or died. Nothing could stop Snitch from killing him, apart from the fear that Devil would pull the trigger without caring that in the next breath he'd have been dead.

After Snitch had pulled the gun away laughing, Devil had reached down, grabbing the girl. He'd taken her out of Fort Wills away from the wretched life waiting for her back home. Every now and then he made a few calls, making sure she was safe, looked after, and taken care of. On his last call he'd discovered she was a married woman with three teenage boys. She thanked him for the life he'd given her.

Pushing the thoughts aside, Devil came back, staring at his cock inside Lexie's body. She hadn't moved since the spank he'd landed on her rear. Teasing her clit, he waited for her to make a move. It wasn't long before he was blessed with her thrusting against him. Once she started moving, thrusting on his cock, he lost all thought for anything else.

Her cunt tightened around him, and he felt each new wave of cum surround him. The sensation was fucking magnificent.

"Come for me, baby," he said, leaning down to kiss her back.

Stroking her clit, he slowly withdrew from her pussy only to glide back inside. Each time he felt the tip hitting her cervix, making her moan.

His woman loved a little bite of pain.

Pinching her clit, he ran his fingers over her clit prolonging her pleasure.

"Please, Devil. Don't tease me."

"You're talking to the devil, baby. All I ever do is tease."

However, he wanted to do more than finger her. His teasing ceased, and he started to caress her clit.

Her peak drew nearer. He heard her gasps along with feeling the tightness of her pussy.

Closing his eyes, he sent her over the edge feeling, hearing, and relishing the sounds of her orgasm. Lexie let him have it all without holding anything back.

When she was finished, he gripped her hips, pulled out of her heat only to slam back inside. He was relentless as he fucked her hard. Through it all he stared at the tight hole of her anus.

Pulling out of her, he slid two fingers inside her pussy getting them slick. Once they were wet, he replaced his fingers with his dick once again.

Sliding his wet fingers against her ass, he pressed on that puckered hole. She tensed up, but he kept up his thrusts, waiting for her to relax. The last thing he ever wanted to do was hurt her.

Devil wanted to give her the entire world. No woman, not even Lash's woman, had ever inspired such good feelings inside him. For so long women had become a source of fucking. They gave him a release his body needed, and for it, he gave them money or a good time.

"Devil?" She glanced over her shoulder at him.

"Don't you worry about a thing, baby. I wouldn't do anything that would hurt you." Stroking the base of her back, he returned his gaze back to his fingers. Using the tip of his index finger he slid the tip inside, her muscles fighting to keep him out.

Earlier in the week he'd already picked up some lubrication from the sex store near the strip club. He kept it in one of the drawers beside the bed. Devil wasn't in the mood to leave her pussy. The urge to fill her with his cum was too fucking strong, which surprised him. He hadn't bothered buying any rubbers, and the thought of Lexie getting the morning after pill riled him.

There was no way she would be killing his baby. He wouldn't have it. Devil refused to let her even think about it.

"You feel the burn, Lex?" he asked, going deeper into her ass. He paused in his fucking, wanting her to want it as well.

"Yes." She whimpered, yet slowly, her body started to relax, giving in to what he wanted to do.

Smiling, triumphantly, he fingered her ass and claimed her pussy at the same time, working both holes together in harmony.

Lexie soon took over, thrusting back against him, begging for more.

There was a knock at the door, interrupting them.

Devil paused as he listened to someone try the door. "What the fuck do you want?" he asked.

"They're all out of burgers," Judi said.

He felt Lexie tense at the sound of Judi's voice.

"They told me to come and ask you as you wouldn't bite my head off like you would theirs."

His men were fucking pussies. They sent a teenager to do a man's job.

"They're in the fridge," Lexie said, shouting up for Judi to hear.

"Okay, do you want some saving?" Judi asked.

Running a hand down his face, Devil actually felt himself blush. With his cock in Lexie's pussy and his finger in her ass, he couldn't believe he was talking to the girl through the bedroom door.

He hoped she hadn't been listening to them screwing for too long.

"Yeah, make sure none of those dipshits leave, either."

"Will do. Have fun."

He heard Judi walking away, humming to herself. His cock hadn't lost any of its hardness.

Lexie giggled. "I hope she didn't hear anything."

"Me, too." Rubbing her back, he waited for his heart to stop pounding from the interruption. "My boys did that on purpose."

"What are you going to do?" she asked, glancing at him.

"I'm going to kick every one of their scrawny asses."

She laughed. "She's doing much better."

He nodded. Devil was impressed by Judi's attitude. None of them knew how long she'd been working the streets or how long Rob got his claws inside her. Devil didn't really want to know the answer. He had a feeling that once he knew the truth, there would be no way he could let Rob live.

Right now, he needed to keep the peace. Jerry promised him that Rob would stop being all that important once he caught up with the little shit.

All of that could wait. Thrusting his finger inside Lexie's ass, he took her hip and started to work his length inside her.

"Together we'll work on wiping everything from Judi's mind," he said. "Kid deserves some peace and happiness, and we're going to see that it happens." He closed his eyes, thinking about Lexie by his side. The image turned him the fuck on. "First, I'm going to fuck you until I fill you with my cum, and then we're going down to the barbeque."

Pulling out of her pussy, he watched himself slide right back inside. Working his finger in her ass, he did the same, working her body, possessing her for his own.

His balls tightened up, and he knew it was only a matter of minutes before he found his release. He pushed a second finger inside her ass, opening her up for so much more. Lexie whimpered, and she didn't fight him. She pressed back against him, and Devil couldn't stop as he held her hip tighter than ever before and slammed inside her.

Over and over he slammed his cock so deep inside. Her moan turned to full blown cries echoing off the walls. The pleasure intensified with every second.

Devil plunged into her one final time as she found her second peak. Their moans mingled, and her pussy took every bit of his cum. When they were finished both had a nice sheen of sweat over their skin.

Removing his fingers from her ass, he moved to the en-suite bathroom, washing his fingers and returning with a cloth. Lexie lay collapsed on the bed.

"I can't move."

"You can move, baby." He wiped her ass,

cleaning away his excess cum, which was dripping from her pussy.

They changed back into their clothes, and together they walked out toward the barbeque. Devil kept hold of her hand even as he grabbed a beer. The men noticed his possession, but he didn't give a fuck. Their smiles, however, pleased him.

From the looks on their faces, he knew they were happy for him to settle down.

Chapter Nine

Lexie felt really brave. She didn't know how she could have been fucking Devil when Judi asked about the burgers and then come down to face the other girl. With Devil holding her hand, she figured he didn't give her much of a choice. He handed her a beer, which she accepted. She took sips not wanting to lose her head about anything.

The men were all giving her knowing smiles. Ignoring them was not an option. Then Devil grabbed her around the back of the neck, pulled her close, and claimed her mouth.

She heard him mutter the words "old lady" to his men. Lexie wasn't sure what the words meant, but the teasing left their gazes easily. Frowning, she saw something similar to respect coming off them.

Squeezing his hand, she left his side to find Judi. The younger girl was studying in her book, writing notes, drinking some juice. She looked so damn young. Her gaze looked up to meet Lexie's. Judi simply smiled at her. There was no condemnation in her gaze or judgment.

"Hey," Judi said.

"Hey."

"The food is going thick and fast. Devil's boys know how to eat. Next time I think you should order twice as much."

Glancing toward the barbeque she saw Curse had taken over flipping more burgers. The pile of buns on the table had diminished as well. Lexie made a note to buy more for the next barbeque.

"How are you doing?" she asked, returning her attention back to Judi.

"I'm good. I think I'm going to ace the history part of my exam. I'll struggle with math, though. Never been too good at math." She sucked from her carton of juice.

"I'm really sorry about what you heard," Lexie said. There was no way she could leave anything unsaid or unfinished with Judi. She really did enjoy having the other girl around.

"I didn't hear anything bad, Lex."

She noticed Devil and Judi called her either Lexie or Lex, depending on their mood. Was the young girl trying to make her feel at ease?

"Look, I'm really sorry. I know it must be hard for you after everything that happened."

Judi dropped the book, her frowning gaze directed at Lexie. "Do you like Devil?"

"What?" Lexie asked.

"Devil, do you like him?"

Looking toward where he stood. Simon was in his arms looking around the garden. It was like Devil had never *not* been there. Simon took to him faster than Lexie understood. Did the little boy know the man was his father?

"Yeah, I like him."

"I don't know everything that happened, but I know Simon isn't your son." Judi's words cut Lexie deep. She knew Judi wasn't being mean by her words, only speaking the truth.

"He's my, erm, he's my sister's son."

"Devil doesn't care about her, Lex. I can see it the way he looks at you. You're so right for each other. I hope you can see that."

She quickly looked back to see Devil watching her. Raising her beer, she saw he raised an eyebrow before looking down her body. She felt his touch from his gaze alone. The heat within his depths reminded her that less than an hour ago he'd been pumping away inside her, giving her one of the most amazing orgasms she'd ever known.

Turning back to Judi she saw the young girl smile. "See, he's lovely."

"I think you're the only one I know who sees him and the whole club as lovely." Tucking some hair behind her ear she smiled at the young girl.

"He did for me what no one has ever done before. He fought for me. I've never known what that would be like at all." Judi gazed down at her books. "I thought my life was over. Rob…" She stopped talking to run her hand down the spine of her course book. "He took everything away from me. He made me feel like scum." Tears were shining in Judi's eyes. "I had no one but him and the beatings he liked to give me."

Lexie hadn't known the truth behind what had happened. She asked the young girl why Rob was beating her.

"He took me to one of the houses—" She stopped to point up and down the garden.

"In this street?" Lexie asked, shocked.

"Yeah. One of the men wanted a bit of fun. When he saw me he asked how old I was. He didn't like my age and kicked me out of the house. From what I saw, he started to hit Rob, in the ribs, not in the face. Told him to take me away and learn what real women were. I didn't know his name. Then when we got back to the apartment block, I was taken by three different men in cars. They all wanted something different but refused to pay. Rob wanted his money. He only ever wanted the money I earned."

"Did you see any of your own money?" Lexie asked.

"No. He took it all. I got a shopping bag each week of food. I wasn't allowed anything else at all." The tears were sliding down Judi's eyes. "I don't think I can do this." Moving to the sun lounge that Judi was sitting on, Lexie pulled the young girl into her arms.

"We've got you, and nothing is ever going to happen to you." She held her tightly. None of the men approached even though they were watching the interaction. Devil moved a little nearer but didn't close that gap.

"How can I go to school? Everyone is going to know what I was. I could have been with their fathers. Their friends." She sobs grew louder.

"Come on. We'll go inside and have some privacy." Standing up, Lexie helped Judi into the house. The men were watching them. Devil looked ready to commit murder. He really was a softy providing no one got on his bad side.

"I didn't mind what I heard with you and Devil. It sounded like you were having fun," Judi said.

Sitting her at the kitchen counter, Lexie grabbed another fruit juice from the fridge. She paused, looking at the other woman.

"Do you know how much I wished for something like that? I've been with over a hundred men, and I'm not even eighteen years old."

Lexie didn't say anything. She'd been with two men in her whole life.

"How do you know the number?" Lexie asked.

"I counted them."

"We'll get through this together, honey."

"Anyone who attacks your name will deal with all of us," Devil said, entering the kitchen. "The men had this made for you." He lifted up a small leather jacket. Lexie smiled as she read what was printed on the back: Chaos Bleeds Princess. "You're one of us, and we take care of our own. Stand up."

Judi went to Devil putting the jacket on.

"There, no one will mess with you. I get angry when I don't get my own way. Just you watch. You're a Chaos Bleeds member."

Lexie fell for Devil right then. She had liked him, but in that moment where he was being really nice to Judi, she truly fell in love with him. He was so sweet and tender.

In no time at all the rest of the boys had pulled Judi out. Just watching them with her, Lexie could tell they made her feel like a princess.

Devil grabbed several beers from the fridge.

"What are you doing?" she asked, washing up the plates. The barbeque was long finished, and the sun was setting. The strong ambers and intense colors were shooting across the sky.

"Having a few beers with the boys. They'll be staying the night here," he said, tugging her close to press his lips to hers. "You'll be with me. Come on out."

Simon had been settled down, and Judi was in her room, reading.

Heading out with Devil, she sat on his lap as the men started playing cards.

"You're all a bunch of pussies," Devil said.

Lexie laughed, knowing he'd been waiting for the right moment to tell his men what he thought.

"What?" Ripper asked.

"Sending a girl to do your job. I didn't realize the kind of cowards I rode with," Devil said.

"We weren't wrong. You'd have castrated us for interfering with your fun." This came from Curse.

They talked amongst themselves as Lexie thought about the young girl in the house. "You were good with Judi today," she said when they stopped arguing.

"She's a sweet kid. The bastard took too fucking

much from her." His fingers stroked along her thigh. The denim didn't stop the pleasure she experienced from his touch.

"Did you hear what she said about one of the men wanting her along this street?" she asked.

"Yeah, I heard. I also heard that he didn't do anything to her. Man was looking for a woman, and Rob handed him a girl. Judi's been through too much, and I think it's time for her to know what it's like to be a kid. I'm not going to cause problems for her, but I'm not going to act like it hasn't happened." His hand moved further up her thigh. The tips of his fingers grazed her pussy with his touch.

"She's a lucky girl," Lexie said, resting against him as the conversation picked up. He kept a firm hold of her throughout it all.

For the next hour she tried not to moan aloud as his touch became more daring, touching her blatantly in front of his men. None of them made a comment, but she saw them watching.

"So, boys, what do you think of staying in Piston County?" he asked.

Lexie tensed, wondering if she was about to hear them start disputing their stay.

"Club is coming around. I can see us setting down roots. I don't think we should be moving Judi around, and she's one of us now," Curse said. "I'm ready to stick around with Vincent."

Several other men voiced their positive thoughts. She felt giddy at their words. Devil was staying.

You're falling.

No, she wasn't fucking falling. She was already there, loving him.

"Then we're staying." Devil lifted her up off his lap, finishing off his beer. His arm was still around her waist. "Keep it quiet, and don't drink too much. I don't want Judi uncomfortable."

"Dude, we're being pretty fucking sweet for you," Death said.

She didn't want to know why they got their names. Death sounded way too scary.

"Good. See you in the morning." Devil kept his arm around her as they headed toward the house.

****

Devil stroked her stomach as he made his way upstairs. Lexie didn't push him away, and he kept a firm hold of her. Her body was so soft against him. The way he saw her with Judi made him feel so fucking proud. She didn't hurt the other girl but embraced her as if they were sisters. There were times he felt Lexie was a lot older than she actually was. The only way he could think to describe her was very motherly.

Between Simon and Judi, Lexie was a natural in caring about everyone. He'd watched her working the kitchen, cleaning up the house and dealing with the kids. The house was perfect, and he found himself calming down within himself merely watching her.

Closing and locking the door, he spun her in his arms.

"Do you have a problem with us staying around?" he asked. He had felt her tense when he asked the boys.

"No, I don't have a problem with that at all." She wrapped her arms around his neck, tugging him down. "In fact, I like it. I like it a hell of a lot." Her lips covered his, and Devil realized it was the first time she initiated a kiss between them. Holding onto her plump ass, he rubbed his cock against her pussy.

"What has gotten into you?" he asked.

"Nothing. I just realized I liked you." She kissed down his cheek to his neck. Off his jacket went, followed by his shirt. "I love your tattoos."

Her fingers skimmed down his chest then up his arms before stopping around his neck. Stroking her cheek, he moved down to sink his fingers into her hair. The length flowed down her back. Fisting the length he watched her gasp and her eyes dilate.

"I'd love to have my name tattooed over this lush, tight body." He tore the vest from her. The material tore with the force of his grip.

She squealed. "You're ruining my clothes."

"If we didn't have company I'd have you running around naked all day long."

Her lips pressed to his chest as her hands worked down to his jeans. Releasing her hair, he removed her bra letting those full tits swing free. Devil was addicted to her tits. Fuck, he was addicted to her body. The ripe curves were practically begging to be touched.

Lexie went down to her knees in front of him. She opened up his jeans, peeling the fabric down his legs. He stepped out of them, kicking them aside along with his boots. Devil never wore any underwear. He didn't like the feel of the fabric around his dick.

She wrapped her fingers around his length, and with the other hand she cupped his balls. Gritting his teeth, he forced himself not to grab her, fling her to the bed, and pound into her tight, hot cunt. Devil had other plans. All day he'd been admiring her ass, and earlier had only driven his need up high to feel her tight ass wrapped around his dick.

"What you going to do, baby?" he asked.

"You're so long and big." Her fingers ran from the root to the tip of his cock. He fingered the long strands of her hair as she stared at his shaft.

"Are you just going to stare at me all day, or are you finally going to put those lips to good use?"

Her fist tightened around his shaft making him moan. The grip on his balls remained the same. She still wore her jeans, and that was too many clothes for his liking.

"Well, if all you're going to do is look your fill then I think it's time to get this ball rolling." Grabbing her arms, he carried her to the bed, flinging her on top. She bounced, squealed, and he tore at her jeans before she got the chance to fight him.

"You're insane," she said, giggling.

The panties went with the jeans. Lifting her pelvis up to his mouth, he covered her pussy, sucking on her clit. He heard her cry out. Tonguing her clit, he sucked the nub into his mouth. The taste of her cum exploded on his tongue. He moaned, flicking her tongue as he pressed a finger inside her.

She wrapped her legs around his neck, and he worshipped her pussy.

"Fuck, please, Devil, let me come."

He caressed her clit driving her closer and closer to orgasm with every passing second.

Her pussy gripped his fingers. Turning them inside her, he stroked her g-spot. She cried out, and he lapped at her pussy. She shattered within seconds, coating his fingers with her cream. He continued licking her until she could take no more. Lowering her to the bed, he left her side to grab the lubrication from the drawer. He placed the tube on top of the drawer so he could grab it with ease.

Lexie sat up on the bed, smiling at him. The smile was so fucking sweet, and it struck him right in the heart. This woman was going to be the death of him if he wasn't careful. Her finger stroked down his chest going toward his cock. He felt the blood leave his brain as it swamped his cock. Glancing down, he saw the evidence throbbing at him. Devil was so close to the edge.

"You can't tease me, baby. Remember, I'll always pay you back."

She climbed off the bed, taking hold of his hand as she did. She turned him to the bed, pushing him to a sitting position. He opened his legs giving her plenty of room to crouch down to get what she wanted. Her hands ran up and down his thighs, driving his need higher. Stroking the silky length of her hair, he waited for her to take him.

Devil didn't have to wait long. Lexie took the tip of his shaft between her lips. She licked the tip, swallowing down his pre-cum. Soon, she sucked her cheeks in taking more and more of him into her mouth. Closing his eyes, he enjoyed the feel of her warm, wet mouth enveloping him in.

"Fuck that feels good," he said.

She took more of him until he hit the back of her throat. He gripped her hair tighter as he didn't want to feel her gagging on his length. He wasn't interested in hurting her. Lexie didn't force the issue, taking only so much. She covered the base of his shaft with her hand. Her lips only went to where her hand lay around his shaft. She worked her mouth and hand in time. The movement drew him closer and closer to orgasm.

He knew this wasn't how the night was going to end. Devil had his plans cemented, and no amount of cock sucking was going to change that.

When he had enough, he pulled her off his length and placed her back on the bed on her knees. She glanced at him smiling. "I think you've got a thing for my ass."

Devil slapped her rounded cheeks hearing her squeal. "I love your ass, baby, but remember I promised you I'd own your cunt, mouth, and ass. It's time for me to claim your ass."

He opened the tube of lube he'd put on top of the drawer. His shaft stuck right out, red and throbbing. Devil coated his cock with over half a tube of lubrication. The porno movies had it wrong when you only saw the guy spit on his hand or the woman salivating over the shaft. In all of his experience, plenty of lubrication was a given in having anal sex.

With the other half of the tube, he squirted the rest onto her ass. She gasped as the lube had a slight chill to it.

"I'll warm it up for you, baby. I promise." Throwing the empty tube away, he concentrated his efforts on her ass. Sliding his fingers through the crack, he coated his digits with the lube before pressing more into her ass.

She tensed around him, but he didn't let up, sliding his fingers in deep. Once she'd taken both of his fingers, he pressed the head of his cock to her ass. The tight muscles stopped him from going any further. Pressing more against her ass, he waited for her to relax. After several seconds passed, Lexie finally relaxed long enough for him to slide the tip inside. Returning his hands to her hips, he fed his cock into her tight, hot ass.

Their moans mingled together, echoing off the walls. She collapsed to the bed so only her bottom half was raised on her knees.

"How are you feeling, baby?"

"Fucking wild. You're in my ass."

He laughed, keeping his grip on her hips.

"That I am, and it's about to get a whole lot fucking wilder." He pulled out of her ass, watching himself appear. Without waiting for her to grow accustomed to him not being inside her, he slammed back in. She cried out. Her ass tightened around him.

Over and over, he fucked her ass, all the time

wanting to brand her body with his cock. He felt possessed with the need to fuck her harder.

"Stroke your clit," he said. "I want to feel you come."

Her hand disappeared between them. He felt the change in her body the instant she started to finger her sweet clit. It was unlike anything he'd ever felt. Marking her didn't feel enough, and he felt like a fucking brute for the possessive feeling flowing through him.

After a few minutes of her playing with her pussy, she came apart, and her ass tightened even more around him.

Closing his eyes he thrust inside her one final time feeling his orgasm wash over him. He collapsed over her, panting for breath.

Then like a giant wave Devil realized what he was feeling for her.

Devil was in love with Lexie Howard.

Chapter Ten

On Friday night the following week Lexie stayed around Phoebe's house. She'd grown close to the other woman in the last few weeks, and they'd worked relentlessly in bringing the club back up to a good standard for the boys. Judi was staying over as well. Devil's large house was too much for either of them when he wasn't staying at home. Lexie certainly wasn't used to the noises and could only deal with them when he was home. He'd left the house a couple of hours ago telling her that he wouldn't be home. She hated when he left her alone. The last week since their barbeque had been something of a fairytale. For so long she hadn't believed in fairytales whereas now she was starting to think, maybe there really was such a thing. Not the castles, princesses, and princes but something magical within life from allowing others inside.

Sitting on the sofa she smiled at an approaching Phoebe. She really did like the other woman.

"Kids are in bed. Vincent is having some time with his brothers. All is right in the world. At least, everything is all right tonight. I can only handle so much calm," Phoebe said, pouring herself a glass of wine as Lexie finished some juice. She didn't feel like drinking beer, and she'd never been much of a wine drinker.

"I know what you mean. It seems so strange to be sat here drinking wine and having fun," Lexie said, smiling. She felt totally relaxed.

"Well, only one of us is drinking wine. You, you're disappointing me."

"I've never had a liking for the stuff."

"When you've got kids like mine along with a man like Vincent, you'll consider a glass of wine a luxury." Phoebe sipped at the liquid. "Not that I'm a complete drunk or anything. I don't drink apart from special occasions."

"I believe you."

"Thank God." Phoebe sat back, resting her head across the back of the sofa. "It's nice having a woman in the lifestyle. Being Vincent's old lady can get a little lonely at times."

"Old lady?" She had heard Devil mutter it at times, but he'd never actually told her what it meant.

"Yeah, the club who have women they're going to marry are called old ladies. I'm an old lady. Then you've got the club whores and sweet-butts, and their main role is to please the men. Vincent won't be getting any kind of pleasure like that. I'll see to it. I'm always happy to serve my man." Phoebe licked her lips.

"What are these parties about, and I don't think I'm Devil's sweet-butt? I'm just the girl who got his kid."

Phoebe slapped her hand. "Honey, Devil is not the kind of man to get all sentimental on shit like that. He's all about getting even. If he didn't want you, you wouldn't be living in his house, off limits to the other men."

"I don't understand."

"Devil has put the word out that you're his woman. He'll be putting a ring on your finger shortly, and believe me when I say you don't want to know what happens at these parties. I learned at a young age what I wanted to know and what I didn't." Phoebe sipped at her wine, flicking some hair out of her face. She was such a beautiful woman. Lexie didn't know how she could begin to compare.

The way Devil had been with her, Lexie felt all of her doubts evaporate around her.

"I want to know what happens to these parties. It

can't be that bad," she said, sipping more juice. She looked toward the baby monitor making sure little Simon was okay. Judi was doing much better and wore her leather jacket with pride. Devil hadn't been wrong. The few times she'd been in town with Judi, people kept a wide berth of her. It was like an instant repellent to everyone around them.

"Everything happens at them. I've not been to one with Vincent. The group was always on the road never staying for longer than a day or so at a time. I think it's because of Vincent they never partied here, but he told me what happened." Phoebe stopped to take a swig of her wine. Lexie waited patiently for her to explain further. "The places are usually full with girls, booze, and drugs. Vincent never got addicted, but some of the men in the club are. Devil doesn't have many rules, but he's also strict about what he accepts. Some men need it to take the edge off while others do not."

Lexie hadn't seen any of the men taking anything. They must have been particularly discreet about it.

"The parties are a free for all. I'm letting Vincent go alone tonight as it's his first in so long. He's been home and good to me. It's the least I can do. Oh, as an old lady, be aware of your true position in life. You're here to serve your man, but know it's up to you if he strays or not. Vincent will not stray as he knows I wouldn't let him near me if he even fucking thought about it." Lexie listened as Phoebe went on and on. The more the other woman talked, the harder it was for her to concentrate. "Earth to Lexie."

Glancing up she saw Phoebe had been running a hand across her face. Smiling, she rested her head on her hand. "What's going on? Sorry, I missed something."

"You complete zoned out there, didn't you, hon?"

"Yeah. It's you talking about women and the

sweet-butts along with the old ladies. It's too much for me to deal with at the moment."

"Devil not talked this through with you?" Phoebe asked.

"No, we talk. Of course we talk about everything, but he's never actually told me what I mean to him or where we're supposed to go from here. It just seems insane that I'm living with someone, and I don't even have a clue what it all means." Blowing some hair out of her face, she smiled sadly at the other woman.

"I know Devil, not well, don't get me wrong, but well enough to know that he's crazy about you. I mean, I think he's in love with you. Completely, totally in love with you."

Looking down at her lap, Lexie smiled, wishing what she said was true. Her feelings for Devil had changed so much. She didn't have a clue how she'd fallen in love with one of the most dangerous men she'd ever known.

"I don't know where I am with his life."

Phoebe sighed, checking her watch. "I tell you what, why don't you go and see him? The party won't be going crazy or anything yet."

"No, I couldn't go to him. That would scream obsessive much." Her heart was pounding.

"I didn't take you for the giving up type of person."

"I'm not."

"Then go to him. Go and tell him how you feel. You do love Devil, don't you?" she asked.

"Yes, I do." She did love him. Lexie loved him with all of her heart and soul.

"Go to him. Go and get your man."

"Okay. What do I do?" she asked.

Phoebe handed her the car keys. "Take my keys

and get your ass over there."

Staring at the keys in her palm, Lexie left Phoebe looking after Simon and Judi as she climbed behind the wheel. Before she could begin to talk herself out of everything she was doing, Lexie headed in the direction of the club. Pushing the boundaries of the speed limit she pulled up into the parking lot. There were bikes and a couple of cars dotted around the parking lot. The music was so loud as she climbed out.

Don't give up. Get your ass in there and find out what you mean to him.

Phoebe had already promised to take care of the kids. All she needed to do was deal with Devil and his supposed feelings.

Entering the club she came up short when she saw the women dancing on tables. There were only a few, but she recognized them from work.

Ripper approached, smiling at her.

"What are you doing here, sweetness?" he asked.

"I want to see Devil. Where is he?"

"I don't know."

She stared into his eyes knowing he was lying.

"Don't push me." Lexie shoved him out of the way and charged toward the room she knew was Devil's office. He'd been the one to ask her to decorate the room.

Her heart was thumping out of fear of what she was about to find. Licking her lips, she saw the door was partially open.

"Come on, baby, I can make you feel so good." She recognized Tiffany's voice. Devil's voice was muttered. Opening the door fully, Lexie gasped. Tiffany was straddling his lap, leaning down to kiss him. She couldn't see anything else.

He looked up and smiled. "Lex, baby."

"Fuck you, asshole," she said, turning on her heel

and walking away. She heard Tiffany mutter something, but she didn't care to hear it. The bastard had been cheating on her.

"Lex, wait," Devil said, shouting. She slowed down wanting him to explain exactly why that skank was even on his lap.

She spun on her heel. "Is this what you had planned all along? Get out of the house so you could have a cheap, sloppy fuck with a woman infected with all kinds of shit?" Her control was out of the window. Lashing out, she slammed her palm against his shoulder. "I hate you. You asshole."

Storming away, she headed back toward the main room.

"What the fuck? You can't just come in here and accuse me of shit you don't even have a clue about," he said.

"I know what I saw."

"You didn't see jack shit. I wasn't doing anything. I was fucking working to make sure Judi can get into a fucking good school."

She stopped, glaring at him. "So Tiffany, the whore, just happened to straddle your lap, sucking on your neck." Lexie glanced toward his neck to see no signs of him being mauled by the other woman. *Whatever.* The bitch probably got her claws in him in another way. The jealousy was eating at her.

"You worked with this woman. She's not calling you a whore, and you worked in the strip club alongside her."

They were in the main part of the club. The music was turned down or off. What the hell was he saying?
****

Devil cursed his runaway mouth. He couldn't find it inside himself to tell her the truth. Instead he insulted her as a way of hitting back at her.

"What the fuck are you trying to say?" Lexie asked. Her hands were on her hips. She was driving him fucking crazy. Devil had no intention of being in that predicament with Tiffany. He'd not intended to rattle Lexie's cage. The last week had been perfect between them, and now she walked into his club, accusing him of cheating and it was pissing him the fuck off. Their argument had gained the entire club's attention. They were looking between them. The alcohol was flowing even though the bar wasn't officially open.

"Come on, tell me what you think, Devil. I'm sure I want to hear it."

He'd pay for this. Devil knew without a shadow of a doubt that he would pay. The anger in her eyes only cemented what he was about to say.

"You're nothing but a fucking stripper, so instead of running your fucking mouth, come on, Lex, give us a fucking show."

He wouldn't let the flash of hurt he saw in her eyes affect him. His anger was getting the better of him. How dare she accuse him of wanting any other woman but her? Devil hated to admit it, but his dick only got hard for one fucking woman, Lexie.

"What? You don't mean that."

The men were tense as Devil walked over to the music box. Finding one of his all time favorite songs, he let it start. "Give us a fucking dance. You're not my woman, so you don't own me." He was lying more with every second that passed.

She stared at him for several seconds. The animosity pouring from her eyes made him feel like shit. "You want a show? Fine, I'll give you a fucking show." She leaned down pulling off her sneakers.

Standing back up, she threw the sneakers at him,

each one hitting him in the stomach. Devil tensed, and it took all of his effort not to flinch from the harsh hit. Bitch could throw. She stood up onto the beer counter, and the music seemed to grow louder.

The room was deadly silent apart from his men and a few of the women that had been invited over. Their gazes were all on Lexie. She held the room as she pulled the band from her hair.

The long brown strands fell around her as the music took over. Chugging on his beer he watched her hips swinging as the song kept going. There was no lust in her eyes. She wasn't into the dance. Her body owned the song, moving from one beat to another. The harshness of each swing wasn't lost on him.

When she moved off the counter, throwing her shirt out into the crowd with only a bra covering her made him tense. She stepped onto the first table. The men kept it steady. He saw Ripper and Curse were sat both nursing a hard on. Down on her knees she went, drawing Curse up to her chest.

Fuck, he was going to break fucking bones. Her bra was flicked off. She kept the fabric on, moving to the next table before it finally came off. He was getting hard watching her body.

He had to stop it. Around the room she went, removing her jeans until all that was left was the red pair of French lace panties he'd bought her. Devil knew he'd seriously fucked up. This was not how he saw her at all, and he'd treated her like shit. Feeling worse than fucking pond scum, he watched her head toward him. Her eyes were blazing with hatred, and he knew it was all directed at him.

She reached into his pocket pulling out his small knife. The music came to a stop as she cut the fabric in two. Lifting the halves up in the air, she stood in the club room butt assed naked, and it was all his fault.

"There, are you satisfied?" she asked, slamming the panties against his chest. "I'm nothing but a fucking stripper."

With her head held high she walked out of the room by going past his men. None of them reached out to her. He saw in their eyes that they wanted to protect her. Cursing, he left his beer on the counter, following after her.

"What the fuck is your problem?" he asked. Her ass was so fucking sexy, he couldn't tear his gaze off her. His cock thickened remembering how it felt to claim such a perfect fucking ass.

"Nothing, I'm just fucking fine." She didn't turn around to look at him. "I'm just a stripper, remember? I'm no better than a fucking whore."

He grabbed her arm spinning her to face him. "It doesn't sound like you enjoy it at all."

"Newsflash, fuck head, I didn't enjoy it. I never liked knowing men were getting hard wanting to fuck me. Do you know how many men wanted so much fucking extra? A quick fuck here and there? You really think I like shit like that?" she asked, spitting the words at him. He held her against the wall so she had nowhere else to go.

"Why did you do it? You could have any job you wanted."

"No, I couldn't. The only thing I could do was dance so I could take care of *your* son. That's right, Kayla dumped him with me, and I had no one to look after him. I lost my job, and no one else would hire me. I was alone, fending for myself."

He knew all of this, and yet he couldn't stop himself from arguing with her.

"Let go of me." She started laughing, trying to

shrug away from his touch. "You know, I was coming here to see where we were going. I thought there was something between us beside screwing. I was wrong, wasn't I?"

"What do you mean?" he asked, needing her to calm down. He couldn't let her leave feeling this way. There was so much he wanted to say, needed to say.

"Phoebe told me I was your old lady. She said we were a lot more than I ever considered." She looked up, batting the tears away. "I was so fucking wrong about it all. I need some air."

Lexie moved away butt ass naked. Shrugging his jacket off, he handed it to her. "Use this."

She took it without saying a word, heading back from where she'd come. Collapsing against the wall, he ran fingers through his hair. "I'm totally fucked." He'd follow her outside in a second. Heading back to his office he found Tiffany sat naked in his chair.

"I thought she'd never leave."

"Get the fuck out," he said. He'd been so fucking distracted by his work that he'd given Tiffany the wrong impression. Walking to his desk, he grabbed her by a fistful of hair and yanked her off his seat. "I told you to get the fuck out."

She gasped, touching his hands where he held her.

"You don't mean that."

"What is it with women thinking I want something out of them? You ever come near me again, I'll fucking kill you, do you understand?" he asked.

He must have been getting through as she grabbed her clothes and scarpered away. Devil was done with meaningless whores. He was settling down to have something more than a fuck.

Looking outside his window, he saw Lexie

pushing the hair off her face, looking toward the sky. He'd not given it much thought having Tiffany climb into his lap. She'd been there for a second, and he'd literally been about to throw her out when Lexie had walked in, seeing more than she needed to. He wasn't going to fuck Tiffany when he could have Lexie whenever he wanted. Heading outside toward his woman, he found her alone holding his jacket together at the front.

"Have you come out here to insult me some more?" she asked.

"No, I'm not here to insult you at all. What I said was fucking wrong of me."

"It's true. I was a stripper, probably will always be a stripper."

She hadn't looked at him.

"You're my old lady, too."

Lexie tensed, glancing behind her at him.

"I know you don't have a clue what that means, but I promise you I'll discuss it all with you in time. I think we need to get home and just forget about what happened tonight."

His cell phone went off, and he checked to see the caller wasn't recognized.

Ten minutes later, Devil was fuming. Snitch was back, and The Skulls were in danger. His men were needed to right a wrong from his past.

Walking back to Lexie, he wrapped his arms around her, pulling her back against him. "I've got to go for a little while. I need you to promise me you won't disappear."

"You're leaving?"

"Only to handle some business. A friend needs me, and I promised to help him."

"Fine, go."

"Promise me." He tilted her head back to look into her eyes.

"I promise, Devil. I'm not going anywhere."

Seeing she wasn't lying, he kissed her lips and disappeared inside the club. It was time to put the past to bed.

Chapter Eleven

Four days Devil had been gone. Lexie placed Simon on the floor in the sitting room, watching him play. She sat beside him, finding his antics cute. Judi sat with a book in her lap, and Phoebe was in the kitchen making some kind of curry. They were her closest friends. A couple of Devil's boys were hanging around at the club, checking in to make sure she was safe and happy.

He hadn't phoned.

She hated the fact she was sat most days beside the phone waiting for him to call. Closing her eyes, she looked up at the ceiling wishing she hadn't let him leave. What he'd said had been in the heat of the moment.

"He'll be back before you know, and then you'll be moaning and groaning," Judi said, smiling.

"I'm sure he will."

"The boys will be back, and we'll get some normality to this strange world we live in," Phoebe said, taking a seat and sipping at a warm cup of tea.

Running a hand over her face, Lexie wished there was something she could do to make him call. Glancing at her cell phone she smiled as Phoebe made a frustrated noise.

"He'll call. I promise you, he'll be back before you know it."

"Are you really sure?" Lexie asked, pouting. Phoebe had a way about her that made her forget her sadness.

"If he doesn't call then he's got something else planned. Vincent is at the strip club today taking the deliveries for beer and shit. Kids are in school, Simon is playing nicely, and Judi is getting ready for her exam. Everything is all right in my book."

Lexie noticed Phoebe was fidgeting with the edge of her shirt.

"You don't sound all that convinced if you don't mind me saying so." Lexie moved a ball out of the way so Simon could continue on playing.

Judi had her head in a book.

"I didn't get my period," Phoebe said, whispering the words.

"Wow, do you know if it's, you know, the right news?" Lexie asked, lifting her feet underneath her.

"No, I've not said anything to Vincent. He wants to wait a couple more years before we have another kid." Phoebe looked troubled now.

"I'm sure he wouldn't mind. He's, erm, partly to blame." She looked toward Judi, who was chuckling. "Shut it, you." Lexie threw a pillow at the young girl.

Judi collapsed onto the floor in a heap of giggles. In no time at all they were all laughing. During their crazy laughter, the sound of the doorbell being rung invaded their fun.

"I'll go. I'm expecting a delivery of my course stuff," Judi said, getting to her feet.

"I love that girl," Phoebe said.

"Me, too. She's fun."

Staring at Simon, Lexie thought about her own sister. She had more in common with Judi than she did with her half-sister.

"Don't let it get to you, honey. Devil's a good man. Vincent told me what happened. All he did was get angry and lash out."

Lexie shrugged. "I'm not even mad about it anymore." She chuckled, thinking about the heated yet scared expressions of the men she'd danced for. Lexie said as much to Phoebe.

"The boys know they can look but can't touch. I

wish I could have been there."

Looking behind her, Lexie couldn't hear anything from the door, and Judi had been gone a couple of minutes. Getting up from the chair, she walked down the hall and started running as she finally saw Judi fighting with a man.

"Wait, stop." She yelled the words. The man threw Judi to the ground, kicking her in the stomach. "I said fucking stop it."

She flew out of the door and paused as the man she now recognized as Rob grabbed Judi pressing a gun to her temple.

"Get inside, Lex. Stay out of this," Judi said, sobbing. "This is my punishment."

"That's right, whore. This is your punishment for everything that fucker did to me." The hand across Judi's body was bound up. "Took my girl and I'm down fucking money. No one wants to do fucking business with me."

Taking a step closer, Lexie held up her hands. "You do not want to do this. She's under Devil's protection. He'll fucking kill you if anything happens to her."

"Do you think I give a fuck? He rides into our county and tells me what I'm going to fucking do. This is bullshit. I want my property, and I'm taking it. Get down on the fucking ground."

Lexie took another step and screamed as a bullet bounced off the floor near where she was stood. Lexie hoped Phoebe wasn't close by. If the other woman was pregnant then the last thing she wanted was to put the other woman in danger.

"Leave her alone, please." Judi was speaking through gritted teeth. Lexie hated the fear she could hear in the young woman's voice. She wished there was something more she could do.

With her hands flat on the ground, Lexie waited for what would happen next.

"Get in my fucking truck, bitch." She heard some commotion, movement, and then a door opening and closing.

She moved her head to the side, and she saw the guy raise his foot in the air, bringing it down on her back. He didn't use any force, simply laid his foot on her back. "I'm taking my girl, but if anything happens, I'm coming back for you. I just want my woman and what is due me."

When she thought he was going to drive his boot down, he didn't. He got into his truck and drove away. Lexie then heard the sounds of bikes approaching. The car pulled off.

"Vincent, they're here. I can hear them. Thank you so much, baby. I fucking love you." Phoebe was talking over and over on the phone not stopping between each word.

Turning to look at her side she saw Phoebe collapsed in the doorway holding a phone to hear ear. She was crying, clearly terrified. The sound of the rumbling bikes coming to a stop made Lexie start to get off the floor. She was so terrified, and her hands were shaking. The tears were falling thick and fast. He'd taken Judi from her.

"Baby, did he fucking do anything to you?" Devil asked, helping her to her feet. Without thinking, she flung her arms around his neck.

"He had a gun. He's got Judi, and he's so fucking mad. I think he's going to kill her." The words poured out of her mouth one after the other. He pulled her back, cupping her face.

"I'm not going to let anything happen to her. I

promise, baby, but I've got to go. I've got to take my boys and get her before he does something fucking stupid."

She covered his hands where they held her face. Part of her wanted to beg him not to leave, but the sane part knew Judi would be dead if he didn't go.

"I need you to be fucking strong for me and for little Simon." He slammed his lips down on hers. "I'm coming back for you, baby. I love you."

Lexie gasped. His lips were back on hers before she could say anything.

"Think about that while I'm gone. I've done my shit, Lex. I'm not going anywhere. I'll be home from now on." He kissed her again, pressed his forehead against hers, and was gone. She watched him walk away as Phoebe walked up behind her, wrapping arms around her.

"They're going to get her, and she'll be safe, honey," Phoebe said.

She wasn't listening. The only people she cared about were Devil and Judi. One moment they'd been laughing having fun, and then Rob had ruined everything.

He loves me.

Lexie couldn't think about that right now. All she could think about was the danger he and Judi were in.

Vincent drove up seconds later. He ran toward Phoebe, pulling her in his arms. "Are you all right, baby?"

"Yes."

Going back inside the house she pulled Simon into her arms, holding onto him, hoping and praying his father would be all right.

"Devil will get her back," Vincent said, kneeling in front of her.

"I know he will."

He rubbed her knee offering her comfort. It meant nothing to her. She smiled, wanting to go back to an hour ago when Phoebe suggested going shopping. If they were out then Rob wouldn't have been able to target them.

"I know Devil. He'll be back before you know it."

****

The truck was in his sights. Grabbing his cell phone Devil dialed Jerry's number. He wasn't going to be handing the bastard over to him. Rob was dead from the shit he'd just pulled. Devil couldn't wait to put a bullet in the bastard's brain. His men were right behind him ready to die to take out this fucker. Judi was their girl, their princess, and no one was taking her away from them.

"What?" Jerry asked.

"Rob's taken my fucking girl. Judi, she's not even eighteen, and he's dead."

He heard Jerry curse over the line. "Fucker. You sure it's him?"

"Got her locked in his truck. I'm following him right now. Hurt my woman as well. That fucker is not going to last the next hour. Do we have a deal on this?" Devil asked.

"Yeah, fine. Kill him and bury him. I don't want him or his death anywhere near me."

"I get the girl as well. She's a Chaos Bleeds Princess.

Jerry chuckled. "Do what you want. I've got a feeling we're going to do very well for business." The line went blank. Pocketing his phone, Devil headed toward the truck. He watched Rob swerve from side to side. Devil didn't get ahead of himself or put his boys' lives at risk.

They'd been riding for the last four days apart from at night. After the confrontation with Snitch, working with Tiny, he was exhausted. All he had wanted to do was come home, wrap his arms around Lexie, and forget all about the fucking world outside. Instead, this drug dealing fucker thought he could take Judi.

The last few days hadn't put him in the best of moods, and all he wanted to do was hurt this fucker who thought they could get away with taking one of their women. Judi was one of their women.

None of them stopped or gave any sign of letting up. Devil wouldn't be leaving the truck until he had Judi on the back of his bike. Vincent would take care of his woman, as would Phoebe.

For over an hour they drove until finally, the truck pulled up outside of an apartment block. It looked abandoned. Climbing off his bike, Devil pulled out his gun and waited.

His men did the same getting his back.

"I'm pissed," Curse said, standing beside him.

"Why?"

"All I wanted to do today was fuck the first willing woman who looked my way. Instead I'm following this dead prick around. It's not a good way to relax."

Nodding, Devil tensed as the car door opened. Seconds later he saw Judi kicked out of the van hitting the hard tarmac. A bullet would be too fucking easy for this fucker.

Rob couldn't be all that bright seeing as he climbed out of truck with a gun pointed at them.

"I don't want to cause any trouble."

"Think again, fucker. You wanted trouble the minute you took her. I don't back down from no one." His aim was steady.

Judi screamed as Rob pulled her up by her hair. The action angered him all the more.

"She's just a fucking whore, and she's my little money maker." Rob gripped her tit tightly. The pain showed on her face.

"Please," she said, begging.

He ignored her. Devil needed to concentrate on the man holding the gun at her face rather than at her. Rob had pressed the gun to her temple.

"She's my prized whore. My little earner. Men love her mouth, cunt, and ass."

Devil felt sick. She was nothing more than a baby.

"Boss, end him," Ripper said, walking up behind him.

"You're not leaving here alive."

"No? Then I could always take her with me."

He saw Rob's finger tightening ready to end Judi's life. Devil reacted, firing his gun once. He was always a good shot, and in that instant he proved why. A single hole showed on Rob's head, and he fell to the ground.

Judi screamed, running away as Rob lay dead.

She ran into his arms, crying her eyes out. "I only answered the door."

"He's never going to hurt you again. I promise. He'll never do anything to hurt you." Looking at the ground, Devil moved her to Ripper. "Take care of her."

Leaving her screaming, he grabbed his cell phone once again. He dialed Jerry to tell him Rob was old news.

"Good, the women who were illegal we'll send them back to their homes, well compensated," Jerry said.

"You're not going to exploit them?" Devil asked.

"I'm in the market of making money, not having a prison sentence. Cops and even jurors lose all sympathy when young kids are involved. I'm not risking my life for this kid's fuck up. He thought he could play the game, and he's now dead for it. I'm not shedding any tears. Fucker got what he deserved." Jerry sounded like he was eating on the phone, and Devil asked him what he was having. "Steak. My woman makes a mean ass steak. You should try it some time."

"I'll see." There was no fucking way he was letting Lexie anywhere near this fucker. "See you around." He hung up the phone, then immediately dialed Lexie's number.

"Hello." Vincent answered the phone first.

"Put my woman on the line."

"Devil, have you found her? Is she all right? I love you so much. I don't care about anything else. I just love you."

Her words soothed him.

"I've got her. She's with my men. Tell Vincent to call the Doc. I want him to have a look at her." He looked down at the ground wishing he could have made Rob pay more.

"What happened to Rob?" Lexie asked.

"He's not coming back, baby. I took care of it."

Devil heard her sigh over the line. "Good. We all need some peace. Come home, Devil. I need you to hold me."

"I'll finish up here, and we'll have some quality time."

"I love you, and I forgive you for being a prick."

He laughed, unable to stop himself. "Thanks, baby. I had groveling planned, but you've saved me a job."

She chuckled. "You can spend the rest of your life groveling, honey. Just get done what you need to do and get home. I need my man's arms around me."

Closing his phone, he pulled Rob up off the floor and placed him inside the truck.

"What's the plan?" Curse asked.

"Torch the car. Jerry has a couple of cops in his pocket who'll be paid not to look too closely. He was a pimp, Curse. Fucker caused problems. He didn't help anyone at all. This was too nice an end to his shit life."

Ripper helped him use the gas from the back of the truck to coat the body along with the vehicle inside and out.

"You think he was going to use this gas on our girl?"

"Guy was unstable." Pulling out a cigarette he lit the tip making sure not to go near the truck. He'd light it when he was goddamn ready.

"Lexie your woman?" Ripper asked.

"Is this twenty fucking questions?"

"Yeah, it is."

Looking at his man, Devil smiled. "Yeah, she's my woman. Piston County is our town, and we're going to have a fucking wedding to celebrate."

"Does she know that?" Curse asked, approaching. "I've heard women get pissy when they're not asked first."

"Woman can do whatever she likes. I'm not backing down at all. She's my woman, and she's going to give me what I want." Devil smiled, knowing he'd be groveling tonight.

"You've got some stones dealing with that. I don't know how you can do it," Ripper said, smiling. "Come on, let's get back. I need a shower, a fuck, and then some good food."

Staring at the van, Devil waited for his men to be ready to drive off. Judi would be riding on the back with him. Throwing his cigarette inside, he waited for the flames to start before climbing on. Judi wrapped her arms around his waist, and he drove off toward the house.

Lexie was outside as he pulled up, shutting off his bike. The Doc was already there, and he took Judi inside.

Getting off his bike, Devil wrapped his arms around Lexie, holding her close.

"You're going to marry me," he said.

She jerked, looking up. "What?"

Reaching into his jacket pocket he pulled out the ring he'd bought on the road. He'd been buying a ring when he found Murphy waiting for him.

"Is this a proposal, or an order?" Her gaze went to the ring then to him.

"You can see it however you want. You're marrying me either way."

His men were sniggering. Phoebe whistled. "What a romantic?"

"Vincent, silence your woman."

Next he heard Phoebe's voice muffled.

"What do you say, princess? You game to be my woman?" he asked, challenging her.

"No other women or strippers."

"Already done," he said, smiling.

She looked at the men then back at him. "I suppose I have to. You've not really given me any choice at all."

Lifting her up in the air, he brought her down to his lips. Sinking his fingers into her hair, he held her in place and kissed her deeply.

"I love you, Devil," she said, whispering the words against his neck.

"I love you, too, baby."

Chapter Twelve

Two weeks later Lexie was cleaning away some dirty clothes when her cell phone rang. Without looking at the screen she answered the call. Devil was walking downstairs looking sexy as hell. Her gaze was more focused on his ripped body than anything else. The last two weeks had been insane. The club was working with all the building work completed. Devil had a shitload of cash and knew how to get his builders working fast. Judi was doing much better. She'd been quieter than normal, but she was slowly coming out of her shell.

Rob was dead. Lexie knew she had to be a moron to think otherwise. Anyone who crossed Devil would end up in the ground, dead.

"Lexie, where are you?" Kayla asked.

Frowning, she pulled the phone away and looked at the name. "Kayla?"

Devil jerked, looking toward her. The anger on his face scared her.

With everything that happened she'd forgotten all about her sister.

"I need to see you. It's really important." Kayla sounded earnest.

"Give me the fucking phone," Devil said, taking the device off her in the next second. "Hello, Kayla."

She didn't know what was happening. Scrunching the pair of panties she held between her fists she tried to discover what was going on. His face didn't say anything to her at all.

"That's right. I got to your sister, and I've got to my son. I got the results back as well. Kid is mine. You also stole from me, bitch. Do you really think I wasn't going to find you?" The anger in his voice scared her.

Kayla had crossed him, and she was about to end

up in the ground like Rob.

"Twenty minutes. We settle this fucking score." He closed the cell phone, looking her in the eye. "You're staying here."

"No, I'm not staying here. Not when you're on your way to kill my sister." She followed him as he headed toward the front door. "Devil, you can't do this."

"That woman, your fucking sister, was more than happy for you to be in trouble. She wanted you to take the fall. If I was anyone else, Lex, you'd be fucking dead."

She flinched as he threw the cold harsh truth in her face. "But I'm not dead. Please, you can't kill her."

He turned to her, laughing. "You're fucking crazy if you don't think I'm going to deal with this."

Devil grabbed his jacket on the way out of the door.

"If you loved me, you'd take me with you and you'd keep her alive."

He tensed, turning back to look at her. "What are you saying?"

"I accept your apology, and I don't expect anything else from you. All I ask is you let Kayla live."

"I can't fucking believe this," he said, looking up at the ceiling.

"Please, Devil."

He stared at her for a long time. "Get Judi to watch Simon and get your fucking ass on the back of my bike."

Running upstairs she quickly handed Simon over to Judi. The young girl smiled and wished her luck.

Within ten minutes she was on the back of Devil's bike heading toward an unknown location. She recognized her apartment block instantly. They passed the building, heading down an alley on his bike. They came out behind an old factory. She spotted Kayla smoking a cigarette leaning against the wall.

She looked terrible even at the distance of a few feet.

Her hand was shaking while she smoked. "Stay here," Devil said.

Lexie stayed on the bike. Her heart pounded as Kayla plastered a smile on her face, running fingers through her hair.

"What's happening, baby?" Kayla asked.

"Not going to work."

She cried out as Devil caught Kayla by the hair and started talking to her.

"Devil, stop." He pulled a gun out, pressing it to her head. Lexie realized in the time they'd known each other, he'd never once pointed a gun at her. Fucking hell, what kind of world was she living in?

Covering her mouth, she tried to remain silent as he completed whatever business he had to do.

"You stole my money and tried to keep my fucking kid from me." Her face was pressed against the brick. Biting into her lip, Lexie kept her cries deep inside.

Don't hurt her. Don't hurt her.

"I want you to admit to your sister. The girl who took our kid in without refusing you what you hoped I'd do," Devil said, turning Kayla so Lexie saw her.

Kayla looked petrified. "I thought he'd kill you and be done with it."

The cold harsh truth was like a slap to the face.

"I can't be like her, Devil."

"I know, baby." He threw Kayla to the ground and pointed his gun at her. A bullet went off, but it wasn't anywhere near Kayla. "I was going to kill you. This is your one and only warning. You get out of town, and you do not speak a word of who you are. If I so much as hear the name Kayla Howard I will find you and I'll kill you." He lifted her up, grabbing her chin.

Lexie winced at the pain her sister must be feeling.

"Look at your sister."

Kayla's gaze was on her. Lexie felt under the spotlight.

"That's my old lady. The only reason you're still breathing is because she wants you to be breathing. Otherwise I'd have killed you the moment I saw you." He released her. "Kayla Howard is dead. She died on this day, and she left her young son. Do you understand me?"

She nodded.

"Here's the ten grand you took from me. Get the fuck out now."

He walked back to the bike, climbed on, and they were out of there. Several miles from the house, he stopped the bike. His whole body was tense, and Lexie waited for him to speak.

"We will never discuss what just happened, do you understand?" he asked.

"Yes."

"All Simon needs to know is you're his mother."

"Okay." She wasn't about to argue with him.

"Do you know what I just did?" He turned on the bike to look at her.

"You let my sister live."

"No, I let a person who crossed me walk away. All of my life I've put people like her in the ground. I went to Fort Wills to settle an old score and put the enemy in the ground. Kayla is the first and last person I let that happen with. No one else will get the same kind of treatment."

"I understand, and I won't ask you again." She

rested her head on his back, knowing she needed to keep quiet or he was going to give her a headache with his ranting.

"Good, I want some food, and then I want some sex."

She laughed, holding onto him tighter. "Then get me home."

When Kayla had first arrived in Piston County to hand over her newborn son, Lexie had wondered how she was going to survive with a young boy. Now, she was wondering how she was going to last without him.

Holding on tight to her man, she inhaled his masculine scent combined with the leather of his cut. Devil had struck her from the very beginning. There was something about him that she couldn't deny. He was dangerous, and yet for the first time in her life, she looked forward to the future.

****

Two years later

"You got fucking twins." Devil smiled down at the ground where Tiny's two children were playing with his son and daughter. Lexie was already pregnant with his third child, and glancing toward the pool, he got hard from looking at her. Her stomach was nicely rounded but not too large. Come nighttime he was going to spend several hours loving her body, before he fucked her.

"You fucking start with me and I'm going to kick your ass. I promised to come here for the barbeque 'cause you said you were going to be nice," Tiny said, sipping a bottle of beer. His backyard was full of Skulls and Chaos Bleeds crew. Smiling, Devil felt like the world was his oyster, and all he needed to do was pluck what he wanted.

Angel and Lash were talking with Judi. She held a boy on her hip, looking beautiful. It was funny. When he'd been in Fort Wills he'd wanted her badly. Now, looking at his woman and then at Angel, he wasn't interested.

Judi was back from college. She stood beside Ripper, flipping burgers as his man read one of her course books to her. The woman was studying to be a fucking social worker or some shit. He still couldn't believe it, but he believed in the bills he was paying for.

Every time he signed a check to the school it made him laugh. Nash looked troubled as his daughter sat in the group.

"He got a girl as well?" Devil asked. His life had been chaotic since the last run-in with The Skulls. He didn't want to fight with Tiny and his crew. Devil wanted both clubs to unite as friends, not join forces but be known as friends.

Jerry and his woman were eating and enjoying the party. Lexie was walking out of the pool with Eva. He stopped talking to admire the full beauty of his woman.

"She's really something," Tiny said.

"You better not be looking at my woman."

"I'm not looking at your woman. I'm more interested in mine."

Eva walked into Tiny's arms smiling between the two men. "It makes a change for you two to be in the same place without bashing heads together."

"I know. It sucks, and it's boring."

Lexie picked up their little girl, Elizabeth. "It's feeding time, sweety." She went on her toes, kissing his lips. "Keep everyone company. I'll be back soon."

He watched her leave, knowing he wasn't going to miss watching her feed their daughter. Simon was playing nicely with his toys.

"Will you keep an eye on everything?" Devil

asked.

"You're a horn dog. Leave the woman to feed," Tiny said.

"Go, we'll take care of your boy. Have fun," Eva said, nodding at him.

It was rude, and Lexie would give him shit but watching her nurse his daughter would be well worth it. He found her sat in the nursery with a breast feeding pillow around her waist. His daughter was slowly being weaned off the breast as she was only a year old.

Devil found he loved to sit and watch. He found himself loving Lexie even more as she cared for their little girl.

"You're turning into a slut," she said, looking up.

He hadn't made a sound, but she clearly knew he was there.

"No, not a slut. I just love watching my woman." He took a seat finding the action so sweet. Reaching out, he stroked the baby's head as she took from the nipple. Any chance to see Lexie naked was a joy to him. Her finger held his ring, and her body held his name. She'd gotten the name "Devil" tattooed up her side. The words stood out against her pale skin but filled him with joy every time he saw them.

"We have a wonderful life," she said, smiling at him. "It's why I can never hate Kayla."

"She been in touch?" he asked, tense.

"No, she hasn't been in touch at all. Just think, Devil, without her, we wouldn't be here now." He got up from his seat, cupped her cheek, and tilted her head back. "We'd have gotten here, baby. It would have taken time." Lowering his head toward her, he covered her mouth with his.

She whimpered, opening her lips and giving him more as he kissed her deeply.

"You're going to be the death of me, woman," he said, moaning.

"What can I say? I can't fight the devil's charm." She chuckled, reaching around his head to deepen the kiss.

Devil felt all of his love spill out. Lexie was his heart and soul. He'd started out his life with nothing to lose. No one could hurt him as there was nothing in his life to hurt him with. She gave him a reason to love. Lexie and his two children gave him something to live for that meant for more to him than anything else.

"I love you, Lex."

"I love you, too." She sighed, and that sigh went straight to his cock.

A couple of hours were all he needed to wait for and he could be buried to the hilt inside her. The night time suddenly felt too far away.

Epilogue

Ripper entered the club house with only one thing on his mind, to find a woman to fuck. The barbeque had been great, but watching all the men with women of their own had grown fucking boring. None of the pussy was there. Devil didn't allow all the bitches around his house. There was a place for the women and a place for the keepers.

Shaking his head, he walked to the bar, grabbed the whiskey bottle and sat down. It wasn't long before one of the women joined him. He sat back watching her dance as his cock hardened at the sight. She only wore a mini skirt and a vest top.

The woman was a little on the skinny side, but Ripper wasn't feeling in a picky mood. Some of his other brothers were snorting shit or fucking the women. The barbeque was still going on at Devil's house. Several more of his brothers were still over there. They loved Lexie's cooking and her presence. He enjoyed looking at her as well, which pissed him the fuck off.

In all of his years being by Devil's side, he'd never once poached on one of his women, not even Kayla. However, Lexie made him feeling shit he wasn't used to. Fuck, she didn't even look at him all that much and was only ever nice to him.

Everything going on inside his head was fucking screwing with him. There was no way he was going to deal with trying to fuck Lexie.

Not going to happen.

The woman in front of him touched his junk, and he pushed her away.

"What the hell, Ripper?" she asked.

"Get the fuck away from me."

He walked away from her, heading outside of the

clubhouse. Ripper needed to get his head on straight.
Lexie was off limits, and he wasn't going to do anything
to ruin his life.

When he closed his eyes all he could see was her
dancing in front of him. From the moment he saw her on
stage he'd been smitten.

Going to get your dick blown away.

Rubbing his eyes, he stared up at the night sky
wishing there was some easy fix to his problems. He'd
snorted coke, done alcohol, and still his feelings were
affecting him.

"This is fucking shit," he said.

His cell phone went off. Frowning, he pulled it
out of his pocket and saw Judi on the phone.

"I left an hour ago. What could be the problem?"
he asked.

"I, erm, I need your help. I've done something
stupid, Ripper."

"What?" He went tense. Her tears were clear to
hear over the line. She was all out sobbing.

"I went out for a walk, and a guy stopped beside
me. I think he recognized me from before. I don't know.
He tried to pull me in the car." She stopped crying her
eyes out. "I killed him, Ripper. I killed him with the gun
you gave me."

Shit. Fuck. Shit. Fuck.

Dropping the whiskey bottle to the floor, he
headed toward his bike. "You stay right there. I'm
coming to get you."

"I'm so sorry," she said.

He didn't say anything else. The only other
person he really cared about was Judi. She was such a
sweet girl, and she'd just celebrated her twentieth
birthday. This shit should be far behind her, but instead,
it was right in front of her.

Ripper would do everything to care for her. Turning the ignition on, he headed in the direction of where she was. Helping Judi was in his blood, and he wouldn't let anything happen to her.

The End

www.samcrescent.com

BESTSELLING BBW ROMANCE
SPICY ROMANCE FOR REAL WOMEN

EVERNIGHT PUBLISHING ®

www.evernightpublishing.com

CPSIA information can be obtained
at www.ICGtesting.com
Printed in the USA
LVHW100243200722
723946LV00010B/68